Congratulations,

Miss Scottsdale 2010

Best of Luck at Miss Arizona!

Dusty
Thompson

A Gone Pecan

Dusty Thompson

AuthorHouse™
1663 Liberty Drive
Bloomington, IN 47403
www.authorhouse.com
Phone: 1-800-839-8640

First published by AuthorHouse 10/15/2009

ISBN: 978-1-4490-3741-3 (e)
ISBN: 978-1-4490-3742-0 (sc)
ISBN: 978-1-4490-3743-7 (hc)

Library of Congress Control Number: 2009910642

Printed in the United States of America
Bloomington, Indiana

This book is printed on acid-free paper.

For those who would like to donate to the
Thompson Scholarship for Student Leaders at
Southwest Mississippi Community College
please contact
SMCC Office of Institutional Advancement
601-276-2000

To the memory of my mother,
Catherine Waynette Thornton Thompson

If Heaven has a Sunday School,
I'll bet you she's in charge

Acknowledgements

I want to thank a few individuals who helped make this book what it is. My sister, Shontyl, for reading this about forty-twelve times and still finding it funny. Christopher for being my very best friend and convincing me that people actually did want to hear what I had to say, even if I was pretending to be a 55 year-old woman. And friends and family who read this book in its many incarnations and gave me great feedback and, sometimes, tater tots: Marion, Angie S., Paul, Neal, Georgine, Dr. Pieschel, Paige, Renee, Ross, Pam, Kiley, Kiley's sister's boyfriend (sorry, I forgot your name, but you compared me to Don DeLillo, so you get a shout out), Doug, Daddy, Miss Annette, Marilyn, Lori R. and Jackie.

Cast of Characters

I decided to include a list of people mentioned in this book just so you can keep it all straight, seeing as you're not from here. They are in order of appearance.

Crespo Peterson – Drives a pulpwood truck. Works for Junior Foster. Has questionable taste in clothing.

Belva Jean Avery – Mother of my nearest neighbors, Catfish and Cornbread, and sufferer of post-shotgun injury arm spasms.

Noelicai J. Boddy, PhD – English professor at Romania High School. Part-time poet. Unfortunate murder victim.

Triple J Walker, High School Principal – Self-explanatory.

Finney Boddy – My best friend and soon-to-be-ex-wife of Dr. Boddy.

"Two-Dan" Walker – Somewhat slow and unable to communicate. Witness to the murder.

Ruby MacDonough – Waitress at Tawnette's Wagon Wheel in the truck stop. Gossip-monger.

Tawnette – Not really sure. The restaurant has always been called Tawnette's although I have never been introduced to such a person.

Shaltonia Whipstart – Tattooed hostess/cashier at Tawnette's. You'll see more of her in the next book, *Big Donkey Fool.*

Blythandi Jeskin – Dr. Boddy's teaching assistant. Often mistaken for a gardener.

Elmyra Holstead – My Mother's best friend. Always with big hair. Sometimes nude. Mother of Mary Myra.

Mama Rain Ripley – My Mother. Prepare yourself.

Covaletta Turnage – Mother's nurse and best friend. She died before the book even started. Aren't you the curious cat?

Geneva Landrews – Female sufferer of prostate issues. Do you really need to know these people?

Darmet Hoblain – Member of Romania City Council.

Billy Royce Dobbins – Romania's State Senator. He's in *Big Donkey Fool,* too. It's a doozy.

Mac McIntyre – My husband. Former off-shore oilman and current crochet expert.

Denny and Bailey McIntyre – My precious children.

Kevin Costner – Really? You don't know who this is?

George Strait – If you don't know who he is, then you have to leave my house this instant. I'm not even kidding.

Okay, since you seem to have to know every last person, I'm going to change my list to (1) People you need to remember and (2) people you don't.

People you need to remember:

Harlon Stiles – Sheriff. Father of Gentry. Husband of Velberta.

Jimbo Jakes – Friend of Denny's and a Deputy Sheriff.

Marcetta Steeple – My sworn enemy and the leader of the "Big Hairs" on the Library Board.

Ruetrisha Boddy – Dr. Boddy's sister. A bit on the scary side. Member of a cult…maybe. She might be a Kennedy.

Lolly and Bitsy Keene – 82 year-old identical twins. They are featured in *Big Donkey Fool.* Have I got you wanting to read that one yet?

Hulon "Junior" Foster – Owner of WRLR – the local radio station. Enemy of Dr. Boddy.

Billie Shannon Foster – Wife of Junior. Not a big fan of Finney or me.

DeeDee Smandon – Run for your life. Really, I'm not kidding.

Malvina Jamison – lives near the murder scene. Not to be confused with Javista Farnham or Marcetta Steeple or Deltrenda Walley.

Ti Lashley – Crazy. Rich.

People you don't need to remember:
Jazzy Randy Doomaflatchie – *I'm not even sure this is a real person.*
Joyce Brothers – *I'm pretty sure this is a real person.*
Cornbread and Catfish and Luther Avery
Randa Holley –*Accused kidnapper and local librarian.*
Anne Claire and Jacoby Martin – *Slapee and kidnapee, respectively.*
Marsha Fairfield – *You can try to forget her, but it'll be hard.*
Cindy Birdsong – *You know, from the Supremes.*
Mercy Somerville – *Trash. End of story.*
Maddie LeBlanc – co-owner of the *I Love You Shoppe.*
Jerelyn Fortenberry – *Local attorney.*
LeLe Highsmith-Boone – *President of the Library Board.*

If I said you don't need to remember them, why on earth am I taking the time to tell you about them? Land sakes, I've already written you an entire book!

Chapter 1

When Crespo Peterson's pulpwood truck backfired as he downshifted in anticipation of the sharp curve before the intersection of Nettie Bell Jenkins Road and Forsythe Lowery Loop, it startled no one in particular with the possible exceptions of a few quail in the bushes by the ditch near Belva Jean Avery's driveway and, of course, Belva Jean herself. It wasn't as if Belva Jean wasn't used to the noise, it happened fairly regularly, this being foresting country. It was simply that she still hadn't fully recovered from an accidental shooting when she was eleven. It seems that her brother Dewlap shot her in the forehead while they were doing who knows what, but nonetheless, it happened and the after-effects cause her arm to spasm whenever she either gets emotional, including being startled by any loud noise including something as seemingly unscary as a screen door slammin'. And when she starts to spasm, she goes to wavin' that arm in a circle like she's trying to flag down a car on the highway. And don't even get me started about what happens on the Fourth of July.

Anyway, Crespo's noisy truck also startled someone else whose response made even less sense than Belva Jean's, if you can believe that. It awakened the slumbering academic, Noelicai J. Boddy, PhD, who bolted upright and proceeded to furiously type the opening stanza to what would be, unbeknownst to anyone, his final poem.

"A sacred fear erupts from my bowels,
And causes me to sing,

Of debutantes with golden goals
Of endless Jell-o salads."

He sat back with the smug, satisfied look of those people who don't seem to know they're really big donkeys. His soon-to-be-ex-wife Finney said his ego can be traced to misunderstanding a high school English instructor. He thought she meant that he would be under-appreciated as a poet until after his death. What she actually said was, "You will be dead before you write a decent poem. But if you want to be poor on purpose, be my guest." So he decided to pursue a doctorate in English and impart his wisdom to the unwilling participants in his AP classes at Romania High. No one actually understood his poems, but everyone was quick to call him a genius so they wouldn't really have to discuss anything with him. It was said that an encounter with him induced nausea, from both his poetry and his bad breath.

Why would a man with a PhD and delusions of grandeur teach at a high school instead of a university or at least a junior college? Well, I don't rightly know. Mind you, we've discussed it at great length, just not in the presence of the good doctor. Finney said he was too afraid that people might see through him and know he wasn't talented. I often argued, in my head, of course, that he seemed pretty darn sure of his talent. Whether or not anyone else agreed seemed irrelevant. But that's neither here nor there.

You might be wondering who I am to make these observations. Well, I am the demure Southern belle to be named later.

This latest inspiration was one Dr. Boddy hoped to recite at graduation. Of course, that would more than likely not happen as Triple J Walker, High School Principal, was a man of simple tastes and poetry was not among them; most definitely a poem that could be misconstrued to be about a bodily function and speaking condescendingly of the very norms that we know. I mean what's wrong with Jell-o salads, other than there's just so many of them? Mocking the familiar might work somewhere else, but definitely not here. We are conservative town, at least on the surface. I mean, this is a school that still allows a prayer over the loudspeaker each morning, bless them. I'm pretty sure we don't give one big hoot what the atheists think. Bless their ignorant little hearts.

And I have to agree with Mr. Walker. Graduation ceremonies and bright futures don't come to mind when hearing the words 'erupt' and 'bowel'. However, Dr. Boddy was not to be deterred. He always became a bit wistful this time of year. Whether it was over his seemingly misspent career or the reality of the long summer months in the presence of Finney, for all 24 of the blessed hours allotted in a day without the interruptions of classes, meetings, etc., we couldn't be sure. But believe me, we had a sneaking suspicion it was the latter.

Of course, I'm sure Finney wasn't happy about the idea either. Bless her heart, she had tried her best to overcome their 'new people' status for years and although she was well-liked in certain circles, the poet of the pair, with his previously mentioned breath issues as well as his disdain for 'local color' as he referred to everything except the Sonic and the buffet at Tawnette's Wagon Wheel, kept those circles broken dear friends; irreparably broken. Beyond even the almighty power of duct tape. And you know that can fix anything from leaky pipes and loose bumpers to boot heels and last minute Christmas gift dilemmas concerning those for whom dressing up means wearing starched overalls and their 'good' John Deere hat.

The fact that they've lived in our little town for going on eleven years makes no difference. That's just the way things are around here. Where's here you ask? Well, aren't you the curious cat. We'll get to it in due time, honey.

Over his shoulder Finney stifled a giggle and started singing with more emotion than was necessary, "Don't fart for me Argentina!"

Turning to the source of this impertinence, Dr. Boddy growled, "I can't hone my craft if you insist on caterwauling all night."

Finney continued to sing making up the words as she couldn't remember how to say Jell-o salad in Spanish.

"Besides," he sniffed, "the musical selection is hardly appropriate."

"Excuse me, oh bard of the woods. What musical selection would you suggest to accompany an ode to a Jell-o fart?"

"Oh, how pedestrian, Finney. It is most certainly *not* a 'Jell-o fart'; it's an allegory," he replied icily.

"That is *not* an allegory."

"I have neither the time nor the energy to continue this dialogue. Just go away."

"Gladly," she smirked, "Jeopardy's coming on anyway."

He laughed condescendingly, "As if you'll know any of the answers."

"Number one, just because I don't find the poetry of bodily functions stimulating, doesn't mean I'm stupid, although I did marry you. And number two, if the category is sculptors, the answer is always Rodin."

Dr. Boddy smiled, 'Oh, Finnella, you *do* amuse, but a poet you are not."

"Well, neither are you. That one doesn't even rhyme."

"It's free verse," Dr. Boddy sighed, shaking his head sadly.

"You could have made it rhyme. You should have just said 'ring' instead of salad."

"I prefer salad, it's more visual."

"But a ring could have given it extra depth, like a wedding ring as well as the Jell-o."

Laughing to himself he murmured, "Neophytes."

Finney rolled her eyes, "I think you're weird on purpose."

He looked offended. "Don't you believe in spontaneous genius?"

"I hope you don't think that was genius."

"It's unfinished. I dare not predict."

Her eyebrow involuntarily arched and she laughed, "That's so ridiculous, I don't even know what to say. And you wonder why Junior Foster won't let you on the radio."

"He's an absolutely horrible man. Denying the community access to my musings; how puerile. They might enjoy them. Heaven knows they need some morsel of culture in this rural wasteland."

"You mean, besides chili cheese tater tots?"

"I'm not having this discussion with you if you insist on being rude."

"I thought you weren't having this discussion with me anyway."

"We *were* discussing the inhabitants of this backward burg."

"Why do you hate it here so much?"

"Need I remind you that this "Junior" person has verbally accosted me on several occasions."

"Well, can you blame him? You did get him in trouble with the FCC."

"I only reported the truth. It is my duty as an American and an artist of the highest caliber."

"You'd better leave him alone or you might meet up with a higher caliber. More than likely a .38."

"Lovely, Finney. As you are without a shred of sympathy, I will take my leave and conclude my efforts at my place of work. Graduation is next week and I've plenty to do if I plan to complete this on time."

"On time for what?" Finney asked.

"Graduation," Dr. Boddy sighed, exasperated. "We just discussed that."

"And you think Principal Walker is going to let you read that at the ceremony?"

"If not me, then perhaps a student. I was thinking of one of the Dufresne triplets; possibly Cherry Dee. She's the incoming Student Council President. And she sees my genius."

"Oh does she?" Finney laughed.

"Yes, Finnella," he answered snidely, "There are those who find that I am on a higher plane."

"Oh, you're up there all right."

Shaking his head sadly, he sighed, "Alas, I must be off. I cannot create in this stultifying environment."

"It's just the chicken. You're the one who wanted it cooked in a cast-iron skillet."

"Oh, don't be so literal, Finney. It hardly qualifies as humor."

"You wound me, doctor," Finney smirked as he made his way toward the garage. "Oh, and don't forget to pick up your buddy Two-Dan."

"At least he appreciates my work."

"Another fan, I presume?"

"Yes," replied Noe, "when I read passages, he sits and listens with mute admiration."

"He's slow! I don't think you should count him among the awe-inspired."

"You are ATROCIOUS!" Noe screamed.

"Why, Noey, how pedestrian," Finney smirked.

The door slammed as the voice from the television informed the Funeral Director from Buenos Aires, Texas, "It's your first pick Delroy."

Finney fumed at the closed door and answered, "I'll take asinine poets for $200, Alex."

Chapter 2

After settling into his orange 1977 Plymouth Volare, with the brown indoor-outdoor carpet on the dashboard, Dr. Boddy picked up Two-Dan and made his way the 10-minute drive to the high school, south of town on Highway 37. His drive always took him past the truck stop, where Two-Dan could be found, spending his time just sitting. Actually, Dr. Boddy had to drive out of his way to get to the truck stop, but in his mind it was okay as he was being charitable, he felt. Besides, Two-Dan always seemed to have a ready supply of doughnuts and appreciated the break in monotony. At least, Dr. Boddy assumed he did as he was always willing to go wherever, whenever.

Two-Dan lived several miles outside of town and, although he was up in years – how old, no one knew for sure- he normally walked to the truck stop in the mornings and spent his days eating the free doughnuts and coffee that one of the waitresses, Marthy Stewart, no relation, always sneaked him. He'd sit and watch people from the front corner booth at Tawnette's, the restaurant inside the truck stop. In his typical outfit of tan Carhartt shirt and pants, he would have faded into the background had it not been for the mad splash of color offered by the supposedly authentic Mexican blankets the other waitress, Ruby Mac(Donough), had stapled to the strip of wood dividing the booths. The greens, purples and reds did not really give the Southwestern feel Miss Ruby Mac was looking for, but they were the only thing that made you realize that you weren't eating in a prison cafeteria, part-time hostess/cashier Shaltonia Whipstart's tattoos notwithstanding.

No one seemed to mind him being there and someone always took him home, as he had no relatives to speak of, which is unusual in a town this size. But, he was harmless and quiet, although he would say a few words, usually what he wanted to eat, which was mostly doughnuts. I guess he requested them or he might not have had a choice. Marthy was charitable, but she had her limit to be sure.

Dr. Boddy's befriending of Two-Dan and subsequent requests to accompany him on his trips to school started as an accident. Dr. Boddy had been distracted by a poem he was working on that had something to do with moral turpitude and K-Mart and when he arrived at his office on campus, he realized Two-Dan was still with him. He invited him inside and Two-Dan seemed to enjoy being anywhere but home and so began their friendship. Lately, though, Dr. Boddy had begun to depend on Two-Dan's presence because he felt paranoid, like someone was following him. Maybe he *was* being delusional, he thought. At least that's what Finney always said when he broached the subject. Of course, there was certainly no love lost between them. She was tired of him and only stayed because he couldn't afford to pay for two rents. Even in small-town Mississippi, a teacher's salary only goes so far. I think it's a shame that the future of our country is being molded by people who aren't valued enough by us to pay them more. Dr. Boddy didn't mind, however, he didn't require much in the way of material things. He only needed his poetry, the thought that he was educating the "masses" and the occasional chili-cheese tater tots at the Sonic. Finney, at the beginning of their courtship and marriage, was on board with his philosophy, especially those that involved Sonic. However, lately she always seemed to find a way to mock anything and everything.

He wished she'd listen or at least not make fun of his fears. But she could be right; I mean, who'd really want to hurt a poet? You have to understand that he considered himself a poet above all other things.

Besides Two-Dan's presence giving him a peace of mind, it also gave him an excuse, had anyone bothered to ask, to always have doughnuts in his car. No that anyone ever asked, but he had prepared an excuse in case they ever did. He was defensive about his weight, but never felt compelled, apparently, to do anything about it. Dr. Boddy was, to be polite, a rotund gentleman with a stereotypical smattering of crumbs on his shirt. The only item of clothing on his body that ever really looked tidy were his shoes and I have a sneaking suspicion that it was because nothing could get to them. Finney claimed that he was obsessive-compulsive, but I don't see how. He was so messy. True, he was always washing his hands, but I always thought he was trying to keep them from being sticky. I guess you believe what you want to believe.

I don't think Dr. Boddy really thought Two-Dan would actually be able to assist in case he was attacked, being that he was so little. Two-Dan was about five foot nothing and weighed less than 140 lb. and was old, ya'll. Mother would say he was a "little old bitty thing". Picture Roy Acuff without the perm and wearing a John Deere hat. If you can't picture Roy Acuff, I can't help you.

Whether he was an imposing figure or not, Dr. Boddy found it comforting just to have him around. Besides, he figured who better to listen to his new poems than someone who rarely said anything? This way he could bounce his ideas off someone without any sort of feedback, which was most definitely not required. Had he truly wanted anyone's opinion, he would've posted his poems on any number of websites devoted to poetry. However, the opinions of others never seemed to matter. Dr. Boddy's self-fascination was sustaining. And I say "Bravo!" I would much rather deal with a delusional ego than someone who doesn't have any self-esteem. My sweet boy Denny has always struggled with low self-esteem although most people who know him would never guess that. He puts up a good front and he thinks I don't notice, but he always seems like he out to prove himself to everybody.

Two-Dan also allowed Dr. Boddy to vent his disdain for the locals without any sort of retribution. Finney didn't want to hear about it, because she was always trying to fit in. And although not well-liked, Dr. Boddy had extensive knowledge of the goings-on in the town, through overheard conversations in the hallways at the high school as well as the teacher's lounge and he had a need to share. He had even made up names for many of those he regarded as lesser, just for amusement. Heck, he even had nicknames for people he liked, if he found one that was clever. If you're going to talk about people in a small town, where everyone's either kin to or married to everyone else, someone with no relatives who seldom speaks is as rare as a Methodist preacher who doesn't cut short the Sunday sermon to beat the Baptists to the buffets.

They had been at the school for several hours and Dr. Boddy was sitting in his office with Two-Dan posted just outside the room. Dr. Boddy was making notes for Blythandi Jeskin his teaching assistant. He wanted her to be able to finish the averages for report cards so he could concentrate on his latest creation. Blythandi was a bit strange for such a small town in that she didn't dress like the other girls, but that was one of the reasons Dr. Boddy liked her. Her outfits were a constant source of irritation for her mother, but Blythandi didn't seem to care. According to her, she dressed like the kids she saw on TV (although what channel, I didn't dare ask) and ignored the stares she received in town as well as the hallways at school. Dr. Boddy held a grudging respect for anyone with individuality as well an appreciation of her thoroughness when grading his papers and organizing his office in the one free period she had. This allowed him ample time to devote his mental prowess to scaling the heights of poetic magnificence. Mind you, this is not my opinion. This is what he would have said had he been the narrator. Now, aren't you glad it's me?

Dr. Boddy was so focused on trying to create a line that would convey his contempt for any imagery that revolved around reminiscing and/or friendships so often found in sub-par graduation speeches/songs that he jumped at the sound of Two-Dan's voice. Two-Dan's voice? He hadn't heard that very often. He'd sometimes repeat things that Dr. Boddy said, but never really talked. He could have sworn he heard, 'Macaroni!' What an odd thing to say.

Suddenly an unkempt man burst through the door and Dr. Boddy stared, appalled. No wonder Two-Dan has said 'Macaroni'. That was his nickname for this idiot.

"What on earth are you doing here?" Dr. Boddy sneered.

The man just stared at him and said, "You gotta learn to treat people raht."

"How dare you tell me how to act…you…you…piece of trash!" Dr. Boddy said through clenched teeth. "Two-Dan, come in here, please."

"You ain't gon'talk to me lak that. You gon'pay," the man said.

"*Gon'*pay. You people are so backwards. It's *going to pay*, you uneducated imbecile!" Dr. Boddy mocked.

Two-Dan edged in the door, looking scared, "Macaroni," he whispered.

"I know, Two-Dan. Please escort this…person out of my office." He hadn't mean to start giving orders – he had never done that before. It just seemed natural. Perhaps he had been a Prussian General in a previous life. Mind you I don't believe in reincarnation, but I guess Dr. Boddy did.

"I ain't goin' nowheres."

"I should think that you *will* leave before I call the authorities," Dr. Boddy said, moving toward the phone.

As he rounded the corner of his desk, he noticed the man was wearing dirty work boots. You can always tell a man by his shoes, he thought smugly, smiling at the thought of his own highly-polished wingtips. Of course, when he stood up his stomach blocked his view, but he knew what they had looked like when he got dressed this morning.

Continuing his once-over of the very personification of body odor, Dr. Boddy thought smugly, dirty pants and dirty work boots and…a bat in their hands! Why didn't I notice that before?

Louder than he meant, from the adrenaline of the situation, Dr. Boddy yelled, "Get out!"

"You cain't always git yur way," the man yelled and lunged at Dr. Boddy, raising the bat in the air.

Dr. Boddy tried to dodge the strike but wasn't quick enough. The bat grazed the side of his head with enough force to knock him down. His head struck the corner of the desk.

Two-Dan had long since left the room. Loyalty is one thing; self-preservation is another.

As the darkness started to overwhelm him, Dr. Boddy struggled to clear his head. I know I told Finney I'd leave a clue, he looked around frantically. I told that silly woman I wasn't being paranoid. Why can't people just listen to me?

His clouded mind searched for a clue in the few minutes he felt he had left. He latched onto 'macaroni', the nickname he had given this man some time ago. If Two-Dan knew it, then maybe he had mentioned it to Finney. Had he? If he had had she paid attention?

He looked out of the corner of his eye to see 'Macaroni' gripping the bat for a second swing. Reaching toward the keyboard he hit the '7' for the fourth time as his vision blurred. His final disheartening thought was 'I'll bet this only makes sense to me.'

Chapter 3

"Elmyra Holstead has completely lost her mind!" Mother ranted as she entered my house through the kitchen door, returning early from her weekend trip to the opera in Natchez. "You will not believe what that woman did!"

That's my mother, Alsace Lorraine Metcalf Ripley, whom everyone calls Mama Rain. Well, except for the ladies her age. They don't call anyone 'Mama'; they just call her Rain. She's been living with us since her housekeeper and best friend, Covaletta Turnage, died and left her alone. Daddy died back in 1978, so it's just been her and Covaletta all these years. She decided to come live with us as she doesn't trust anyone with her things because everyone is 'just trash'. Besides, she's afraid no one else could keep the secret of where she hides her pocketbook (in the vegetable crisper – she read it in Erma Bombeck – but don't tell her I told you).

Excuse my manners; I guess I should introduce myself. I'm Cady McIntyre. Actually my full name is Catherine Dyanne Ripley McIntyre, but everyone calls me Cady; pronounced like lady, of course. Normally, my life is about as exciting as canning peaches, but today looked as if it was starting out to be another story.

"What's she done now?" I asked, knowing full well that her best friend has a tendency to commit *faux pas.*

"First of all," she fumed, sitting down at the whitewashed shed door I had made into a table in the breakfast nook, "she shows up in a sundress with a dickey, looking like who'd-a-thought. Then she has the gall to make me sit next to Geneva Landrews, who swears she has prostate cancer and wants to describe the symptoms to see if I agree. Finally, she conveniently forgets to tell everyone that there's been a change of plans and we're not seeing 'Carmen'!"

"Well, what did you see instead?"

"'Oh Caltucker' or somesuch!"

"You mean 'Oh, Calcutta'?"

"If it's got all the naked people", she frowned, "then that's the one. Then she was so moved, she said, that she jumped up onstage and took off all her clothes! Well, except for the dickey; her hair was too big." Mother, although petite (5'2") is a spitfire. She doesn't really look like anyone famous so she's hard to describe. If you were kin to me, I could just say she looks a lot like Great Aunt Frankie, except for thinner, but that's not going to help you one bit unless you're from Jackson, Tennessee, which I'm betting you're not. But if you are, then you probably know. To help you as much as I can I'll just say that she doesn't like "old lady hair", you know the kind that gets fixed once a week, usually Saturday, her wardrobe is almost more fashionable than mine and she is six kinds of crazy when you get her mad.

"Mother, you are making this up."

"Sister (that's what Mother calls me); I could not *possibly* make this up. Of course, all the other idiots with us gushed about how it was so beautiful that you didn't notice the nudity. Well, except for that woman from here."

Velberta Stiles?" I said.

"That's the one. She fainted dead away."

"Is she all right?"

"Oh, she's fine. That hair stopped her head a good six inches from the floor."

"Mother..." I couldn't help but laugh.

She continued unfazed, "Well, I must have a dirty mind, because I saw it all! Pure D trash. Its things like that'll scar you for life."

"I think I'm scarred just hearing about it. So how'd you get home?"

"Well, I left all those idiots to wallow in sin and nakedness and found a darlin' couple in a gift shop, a few blocks away. They're from Magnolia."

"You hitchhiked?!"

"I most certainly did not *hitch*hike," she said. "I simply told them my story and asked to be taken home. They were on their way anyway."

"You could've been killed!" I said.

"They had a child, Sister. It's not like they were truck drivers or murderers with bad breath, although their baby had gas something awful. Good thing I had my perfume with me."

I could picture this little family floating down the highway in a cloud of White Shoulders.

"Well," I said, "I'm just glad you're here in one piece. Are you hungry?"
"I could eat something, I guess," she replied as the phone rang.

It's been said that the four seasons in the South are Almost Summer, Summer, Still Summer and Christmas. And I'm here to tell you it's the gospel truth. I mean, it's supposed to be hot now – it's June – but we've been roasting since even before Mardi Gras and it was early this year. Even I've been sweating like who'd-a-thought and that's not something I normally do, thank you very much.

Well, I said all that to say this, I was expecting this call. It was from my best friend Finney. I would've bet you dollars to doughnuts that she had been fighting with her husband, the Honorable Dr. Boddy and she had. You see, Finney and Noe, that's his first name, short for Noelicai, but he's not Communist or anything, I don't think, but I guess since the wall's down it doesn't matter anymore anyway, right? But what I was saying is that Finney and Noe are normally wound tighter than Dick's hatband on a good day, you know, one of those cold ones in January, but the heat sets them off something terrible. And I just told you that it's hot a good 11 ½ months out of the year, so you can imagine life at their house.

To be honest, Dr. Boddy *is* a bit much. My husband Mac says, "He's got a little lace on his panties, but he's nice enough, I guess." You'll have to excuse him, he just doesn't 'get' why someone would want to be a poet.

I truly don't understand why he and Finney are together. A shared interest in pie a la mode doesn't a marriage make. Well, now I'm just being hateful. But, Lord, they *are* big.

I did ask Finney once, after one of their big fights, why she hadn't divorce him. Although she occasionally goes to church with me, I suspect she's really not Baptist. I mean she does have wine at her house and, hypocrites aside, Baptists don't even drink wine during Communion (or as we call it the Lord's Supper). We drink grape juice, or 'new wine'. It's Biblical. The Catholics can say what they want; I'll let them take it up with God whenever they get through with purgatory or wherever they're supposed to go. I get confused.

Anyway, Finney's answer was that she didn't want to be 'back out on the market' at her age, but that just sounds so vulgar. Finney had just called to talk about a fight she had with her soon-to-be-ex-husband (I guess she is Methodist after all – Baptists don't divorce. Well, we're not supposed to but I'll hush about that) and before I realized it I had invited her over to chat and have a little munch. I forgot that Mother is wound up, too. This isn't an ideal situation, seeing as how they are both a bit high strung. I'd better put on the dog otherwise one of them will be a gone pecan, if you know what I mean. If you don't know what I mean, I'll tell you. Put on the dog means to go all out – like put out lots and lots of food, so they'll be distracted enough not to hurt each other. Physically, I mean. Feelings would be hurt, if either of them admitted to having any. A gone pecan means when somebody's done for, you know, beat up, dead, fired, stuff like that.

I'm sure you've watched enough episodes of 'In the Heat of the Night' to know that small southern towns aren't like everyone thinks. However, my home place, Romania, Mississippi, is fairly run of the mill if you don't count the love triangle at the nursing home that had something to do with an International Harvester tractor that I never quite understood or the double-assault/failed suicide that somehow included a German Shepherd. Anyway, we're located in the southwestern most corner of the state; we aren't far from the river. Some people, who shall remain nameless, refer to us as stump-jumpers, but I suspect it's dirty, so let's just change the subject.

The root of Romania's name is a story in itself and it's a bit on the stupid side, so bear with me. It seems that when it was founded Romania was called Turnbull due to the fact that Main Street was where the farmer's turned their bulls to go to the slaughterhouse. It doesn't make much sense as you normally wouldn't slaughter a bull, but if Miss Malvina Jamison (unofficial historian) says it's so, who am I to question?

Sometime in the 1940s, a truck carrying lettuce from New Orleans to various points north, overturned in the center of town effectively flooding the streets with hearts of Romaine. The headline of the Clarion Ledger read 'ROMANIA (sic) IN BOGUE CHITTO COUNTY'. Just as an aside, Bogue Chitto is pronounced bo-ga chit-ah. Just be glad I don't live in Tchoupitoulas or Shuqualuak.

Our illustrious town elders, three brothers named Hoblain, interpreted the headline as a "direct order from the state capital" and set about changing the name in a closed session of the City Council, which was pretty much them eating lunch in the embalming room at their funeral home.

Everyone decided it was easier to go ahead with the change than try to reason with the Hoblains, so the name stuck. It should be said that the only reason the Hoblains were continually reelected was to keep them off the streets, especially Darmet. Prior to his first election victory, he had been most notable for burning down the bank seven times. The townspeople would just rather not deal with them. And our county residents feel the same way. This explains our current State Senator, Billy Royce Dobbins many re-elections. If we could just manage to get him to Washington, DC, we'd be good to go. Jackson is still too close for comfort.

Now Romania's main industry is said to be wood products. What they are exactly, I couldn't tell you, but there is a big factory outside of town and lots of people work there. Of course, we have farms and dairies and festivals for the tourists, which always number less than a hundred a year. It's just like any other town, I reckon.

We've lived here for years; since Mac and I got married in '76. Our house is about three miles outside of town on a quiet road called, Lord knows why, Pittypat Lane. I fully expect to see little fat women in gingham dresses alongside the road every time I start toward home. And I just love my house; it's so welcoming. From the pillars on the front porch and the fieldstone patio that extends into the yard on the left (if you're facing the house) to the bright green shutters against the light brown stone façade and those big old pecan trees that stand sentry around our yard, I just think it's the most beautiful sight on earth. Now, mind you, it's not two-story like Tara, but I couldn't imagine living anywhere else. And, of course, my flowers and garden just add to it so much. I think Southern Living should photograph it, but then I'd probably start to put on airs and who wants that, so I guess it's enough that I like it and so does my husband Mac. His given name is Merrill Ennis McIntyre, Jr., and he is the only other full-time resident of our home. Our children Denny (Denton Merrill) and Bailey Catherine are in college up north in Columbus (at the W) and South Carolina (College of Charleston) respectively. Mac is an offshore engineer who retired several years ago after being struck by lightning somewhere in the Gulf of Mexico. The insurance adjuster and his oil company couldn't agree if the rig was in U.S. or international waters, so both sides agreed to send him home if he'd stop yelling at them. He has a bit of temper although he has mellowed since then. He spends most of his time making any number of things from 800 square foot tree forts, for our non-existent grandchildren, to afghans and really big messes in my kitchen, drinking enough sweet tea to fill a cistern. I don't mind really; it keeps him out of my hair.

As much as I put on though, I don't know what I'd do without him. This house is already too big and empty. I need to get a dog or something. Actually, we already have a something that Denny swears is a dog, but it's the size of a Shetland pony and answers to the name Goober. How precious. That huge bundle of nerves, slobber and bad breath is usually the only companion I have on my nightly walks for exercise. Of course, that's not necessarily a comfort, as Goober tends to pee whenever he gets emotional and/or involved in a crisis, which could be triggered by something as simple as being awake. I guess I shouldn't judge. I'm the same way, except I don't pee; I eat. I can't decide which is the lesser of two evils. People might forget that you wet yourself, but you can't hide fat. Well, you can hide some fat but that all depends on how much you're trying to camouflage.

Mother's started walking with me at night although she's been having problems with her knees. She says she doesn't care how much it hurts; she's not getting a big butt like everybody else her age, although we're really not sure what age that is. She said she was forty until I turned forty. Now she says she's over forty and you're rude to even ask.

They say music can calm the savage beast, but I'm here to tell you so can dessert and I have some leftover pecan pie we can share.

I think it's funny how they always get the pronunciation of 'pecan' so wrong when actors try to play Southerners on TV or in the movies. It's ridiculous. We say 'puh-kahn', not 'pee-can'. I will admit there are some hill folk who say 'pee-can' but let's not let them speak for the rest of us, okay? Of course, why they can't just get actors who are Southern is beyond me. The ladies of 'Designing Women' have done the best as far as I'm concerned. Maybe we can find an episode on satellite when Finney gets here. It'll cheer her up. Denny swears there's an episode playing at all times of the night and day, even in Spanish. I wonder how you say 'Designing Women' in Spanish. If I said it like Bailey, who does not care for foreign languages, it'd be *La Designing-o Women-o, por favor.* And you don't have to be a scholar to know that's just wrong.

Chapter 4

At least Finney had warned me this time. Most times, she'd just wheel into the driveway, scaring me to death and setting Goober to wetting everywhere. I guess she picked up the phone before she thought about it, otherwise I don't know what Mother would've done.

I had taken the lead time to my advantage and told Mother Finney was coming over. I also tried to warn her about Finney's clothes and make-up and general disposition. Mother has only been living with us for a few months, but has somehow never seemed to cross paths with Finney. I was hoping the promise of pecan pie was sufficient enough to get us through. Finney usually only stayed a few minutes, as she preferred her therapy to consist of chili-cheese tater tots from the Sonic and Kevin Costner movies. I could take those one at a time, but not together. That would give me heartburn something fierce. The chili-cheese wouldn't help either. I may be the only woman my age who doesn't like Mr. Costner, but I tell you what, I just do not. Give me George Strait any day. I know he only made one movie, but that's all he needed to make, I'm here to tell you. I consider him the "one that wouldn't have gotten away had we ever met". Of course, the closest I came to a brush with fame was meeting Festus from Gunsmoke when Nolee sang on the Louisiana Hayride radio show back in high school. I know you're impressed. Of course, Mac doesn't get jealous of my "George Thing" as he calls it; he's got his "Reba Thing".

"Sister!" Mother said nervously, interrupting my thoughts, looking out the side door to the driveway, "I don't want to panic you or anything, but I think there's a gypsy outside!"

"What?" I asked, turning to look. I laughed, "Mother, that's just Finney. She's mad at her husband again."

"I realize that animal may be married to something, although what I'd be afraid to ask, but it's as big as my Continental and it's headed this way!"

"Mother, please. She just called all upset about an argument she had with her husband."

"I never trusted a woman with that much make-up."

"I know this isn't the best time, but please be nice," I pleaded.

"Who do you think taught you how to act? I have manners, thank you," she huffed.

At least Finney has a sense of humor about herself. She'd have to, bless her heart. As I mentioned earlier, she is on the portly side and her makeup always look as if it had been applied by a group of pre-schoolers, with little regard to the natural lines. She didn't help matters by dressing in wind suits with patterns that would startle Liberace. Denny has said that Finney and I look like the number ten when we stand next to each other, which is mean but still kind of funny. I took after Mother, although I'm a little taller at 5'5". I like to think I look a lot like Sally Field in 'Steel Magnolias' but with ash blonde hair; at least that's what it says on the box. I dress fairly conservatively. Not those high-necked blouses and skirts with the kick-pleat sewn shut like the Pennycosts, but definitely demure. (Just in case you're confused, our pronunciation of Pentecostal as Pennycost is what they call a regional colloquialism. Just in case you weren't confused, then never mind.)

I prefer to wear Liz Claiborne because I never believed those rumors. No one can design clothes that cute and worship the devil. Of course, when I'm working in my flowers or the garden, I wear one of Mac's old western shirts and my pedal pushers. I think they call them capris these days, but old habits die hard, you know?

Knocking on the side door, as is typical, Finney entered, and set her sights on the pale blue and peach striped couch in the family room, which is adjacent to the breakfast nook, bypassing the breakfast table and the aforementioned pecan pie I had just pulled out of the pantry. This was bad.

Covering the better portion of the couch, she bellowed, "I'm so mad I could spit!" With the oil painting of magnolias that hangs over the couch, hovering just above her head, she looked as if she were about to be crowned queen at some festival. The painting perfectly matches the couch and the drapes and that is my only criteria for art. I don't care what anyone says, if it matches the furniture, you're good to go.

Turning her attention to my visibly appalled Mother, she smiled brightly and said, "Hi, Mother Nature."

"That's Mama Rain to you!" Mother said icily, trying not to glare, but failing miserably.

Flustered by little, Finney replied, "A thousand pardons, madam." To me she said, "I love old people. They're so cute."

Ignoring Mother's deadly stare and using a talent Southern women have for sliding from congenial to deadly in the space of a head turn, she continued, "I hate him with the white hot intensity of a thousand bitchy truck-stop waitresses!"

"Who?" I asked laughing.

"Who do you think," she said, her face scrunched as if she were eating a quince. Is that a fruit?

"What'd he do now?" I asked.

"Well, my almost-ex-husband called me stupid just because I didn't like his new poem."

Mother interrupted, "What's an almost-ex-husband?"

"We're in the process of divorcing. I can't afford to move out, so I'm stuck living with a self-important poet."

"Sister said your husband's a poet," Mother said. "I didn't believe her."

"Well, he's actually an English teacher at the high school. He uses poetry as, and I quote, 'an outlet for my rampant intellect.'" She rolled her eyes.

"Who ever heard tell o'such," Mother scoffed. "Why were you married to somebody like that?"

"You wouldn't believe how many times I've asked myself that very question."

"What was wrong with the poem," I asked, trying to redirect the subject.

"Well, it was about a fart and some Jell-o salad, if you can believe that. And it didn't even rhyme."

"A fart?" I coughed out my drink of coffee.

'Yes."

Before I could ask, she said, "I don't know why either. But it's not just the poem, Cady; it's everything to do with us." She reached for one of the plates holding a slice of pie.

"Everybody's just got a trashy mouth. Never in all my days," Mother sighed. "And it didn't even rhyme."

"There is free verse Mother. It doesn't always have to rhyme."

"Bull feathers! Poetry is supposed to rhyme. Didn't you learn that in school? Back in my day, all the great poets rhymed."

"Yeah, like Dr. Seuss," Finney interrupted, laughing as she took the last bite of her pie. She must've been hungry, do you hear me? Of course the girl can eat, but I think she may have broken a record on that slice. I mean, she hadn't stopped talking since she sat down.

"Are you making fun of me?" Mother glared.

"No," Finney said. "But the poem *was* stupid. Almost as stupid as his idea that someone's trying to kill him."

"Maybe the poetry guild," I smiled. "Sorry."

"You don't have to apologize. You're a lot nicer than me. I think he's a moron." Standing and taking a second slice of pie in a napkin, Finney turned to me and declared, "I guess I'll go. Thanks for making me feel better." Nodding toward Mother, she added, "I'm sure I'll be seeing more of you."

"If you eat any more of that pie, we'll be seeing more of you," Mother smiled.

"Mother! That wasn't very nice!"

"Don't worry Cady," Finney said. "I have a cousin with Tourette's." She laughed, "You just have to be patient with them." Moving to pat Mother on the head, she said, "Adieu, Mother Weather!" and grandly swept out the door and into her lemon yellow 1977 Lincoln Town Car, the only car, according to Finney, that was worthy of transporting her to and from the Piggly Wiggly.

Turning to me Mother asked, "Are you sure that's a she?"

"I realize you're not in your right frame of mind from seeing Elmyra nude and all, but, Mother, be serious."

"I am serious, Sister. I was watching some Jazzy Randy Doomaflatchie show the other day and I think she might be a travesty."

"A what?"

'You know, a *transvestigate.*"

"A transvestite?"

"That's what I said."

"Mother, I can't believe you. You know that's not true."

"Well, I'm checking for an Adam's apple next time."

Mac came inside and asked, "She been fightin' with Dr. Boddy again?"

I laughed, "Is the sun shining?"

Mother asked, "Now exactly how did you become friends with that woman? Didn't you used to be best friends with Gisela Fortenberry? I always liked her."

"Good mercy, Mother, that was when I was in college. You haven't seen her since I don't know when."

"Doesn't matter – she's good people."

"Well, yes, but it's a bit hard to visit with a friend who lives in Guatemala."

"Guatemala?"

"Remember, she's a missionary. Finney and I met when we worked together at the concession stand at the Band Festival when Denny was in junior high. I was in the Band Boosters and Finney was volunteered by Dr. Boddy."

"Oh, so you were crazy from the heat?"

"No, Mother, we just sort of started talking after we were the only two people working that thought it was hilarious that one of the things for sale were pickled pig lips."

"Lips?! What in blue blazes is a pig lip and why on earth would somebody pickle it?"

"Well, it's actually the entire soft palate and I don't know why someone would pickle it or eat it. I thought it was a hoot."

Mac said, "Yep, that is weird."

"This from a man who eats pickled eggs."

"Hey, pickled eggs are normal. You can get them at the truck stop."

I laughed, "Well, you can get Ruby Mac at the truck stop to, but I wouldn't recommend it."

Mother interrupted, "Well, y'all are a strange match to be sure."

"Oh, I don't know, other than our size and personal philosophy, spiritual life, cooking ability, sense of fashion and level of matrimonial happiness, we are exactly the same person."

Mother raised her eyebrows.

I laughed. I guess we are less alike than I thought. But we're a good team. We balance each other.

"But, Mother, you are nothing like your best friend, are you?"

"I guess Elmyra and I are different. Lord knows we don't agree on the acceptable level of public nudity, so I guess I see your point. It'd be kind of boring to be best friends with your twin."

"Well, Finney is never boring."

"That's for sure," Mother said as she started toward her room. "I think I'm gonna turn in Sister. I want to watch some Golden Girls and read a little before bedtime."

"Good night, Mother."

I thought about turning in myself, but realized it was only 6:00 and we hadn't even eaten. Mother'll be fine; she keeps nabs stashed away in her room. Mac will probably want Sonic or pizza. I could go for some myself.

Sometimes it's good to eat other people's cooking. Plus, it's really hard to cook for two especially since I've been cooking for four for so many years. Mac could easily eat the other three helpings, but I watch his diet for him. I need to keep him around as long as I can; I don't want to be bored and alone in my old age.

Chapter 5

The next morning I had no more than gotten out of bed when the phone rang. The conversation was not what I was expecting and not what I wanted to hear.

I hung up the phone, dumbstruck. "How awful," I said.

"What's awful?" asked Mother.

"Noe Boddy died last night."

"What's so awful about that?"

"Mother, How heartless! Don't you care the Noe Boddy died?"

"Doesn't do anybody any good to get upset."

"You're right," I interrupted, "we've got to be strong for her."

"Who?"

"Finney!"

"Have you been drinking?"

"Mother! You know I don't drink!"

"Well, you don't make much sense either. Why're you talking about death at this hour?"

"Weren't you listening?" I practically yelled. "Noe Boddy died!"

"What in the blue blazes is wrong with you?" she snapped, staring at me.

"Lord, Mother, Dr. Boddy died last night! Finney's husband?"

"My lands, that's terrible!"

"I know," I said. "I wonder how Finney's doing."

"What kind of name is Finney anyway? Were her parents Moonies?"

"No, I think they sold Amway."

"Is there a difference? And I'll mind you not to raise your voice at me; you're not too old to put a switch to those legs."

"I'm 55."

"And…"

I avoided punishment as Mother had decided to 'make an exception, this one time', it being so early and all. We sat down in the breakfast nook and as I poured the coffee, I told her what Finney had said.

Apparently, Dr. Boddy had been at school late and Finney had gone to bed without him, which wasn't unusual. Since they kept separate bedrooms, she wasn't aware of him not being home until she got up to make coffee. She didn't see him so she called his office at the school hoping that he had just fallen asleep after one of his inspired 'bouts with the muse'. When she got no answer, she decided to drive by Tawnette's on her way to the school to see if he was eating breakfast. When he wasn't there and no one had seen him, she drove to the high school. When she saw his car, but couldn't find him, she began to worry. She panicked when she saw Two-Dan down by the concession stand wandering around looking lost, and decided to call the police. Forgetting she had a cell phone, she drove back to her house to place the call.

Once Sheriff Stiles went to the school to check and Finney met him there, he sent her home thinking it was probably just a fight as everyone knew of their volatile marriage. She left, unwillingly and before she made it home the second time, the Sheriff's office phoned her with the news that they had found Dr. Boddy, sitting at his desk, dead. They said they thought he had hit the back of his head. They were sure that it was an accident, but couldn't figure out how he had gotten up off the floor and into his chair before he died.

I was the first person she called before heading back to the school to make a positive identification. After that she said she would come over here, because, well, that's what you do in these situations – you find your friends. I just needed to prepare myself. I didn't know what state of mind she'd be in and Joyce Brothers I am not. I don't know if it's the hair or the psychology. Probably the hair.

I just don't think that I'm prepared to process that scenario. Dr. Boddy – dead. I attend several funerals each year, but not any that are a surprise; it's usually someone that's up in years. And I'm talking, like late 80s or early 90s. Dr. Boddy was almost the same age as me. He hadn't even thought about retiring from teaching. Truth be told, I thought he was a bit much at times, but he was still a productive person. Nobody liked his poetry, but he sure wrote a lot of it. Doesn't that count for something?

I mean, do you even have to be contributing to society to be allowed to live. I don't really do anything more than volunteer at the library and teach Sunday School. I write letters to some missionaries in Guatemala, but that's because we've been friends since college. Is that enough to deserve to be here?

And Finney said she thought he might have been murdered! Let's not forget about that. Things like that just don't happen around here. I mean 'In the Heat of the Night' is just a show. We haven't had a murder since I can't remember when. Oh, I just don't know about the world today. What's gotten into everybody? People just killing people for no good reason. Dr. Boddy never did anything to anyone that I know of. Least not anything to kill him for.

Whatever I was feeling, I'd have to put that aside and be strong for Finney. She would need a shoulder to cry on, I guess. I know she hasn't particularly cared for him for the last several months, but surely they had to have been in love at some point. Then again, there's that song that says there's a thin line between love and hate. I couldn't imagine ever falling out of love with Mac. Maybe I'm old-fashioned. Or maybe I'm just right and everybody else has gone crazy. Well, I'll get off that soap box because nobody needs that right now, I think we can all agree.

But you have to admit, people get married at the drop of a hat these days. Not that I'm putting Finney in that group, but how *do* you fall out of love with somebody? I wasn't head over heels the first date I went on with Mac, but we had fun and I wanted to get to know him better. We dated for almost 2 years before we got engaged and Mother and Daddy were still not happy about it, I guess because I quit going Mississippi College up in Clinton and college was a rarity back then, especially for farm folk. But I was in love. By that time, I *knew,* you know.

Maybe it's because we've spoiled our kids. We made marriage seem easy because we wanted them to look at us as role models. We didn't really show them the hard work that it takes to keep a marriage strong. Patience and love and faith in God; that's what'll keep you together. Plus, living together before marriage, well it just wasn't done back then. Leastways, not by anyone I knew and most definitely not by any Baptists. Now, don't get me wrong, there are backsliders in every denomination, but I think Baptists feel the guiltiest. I don't care what anyone says, Baptists can bring down some serious shame and guilt, do you hear me?

And I don't mean to get off into religion, but I think its part of the reason people are crazy these days. Murder, rape, divorce, drugs. We just didn't have that in my town in my day. And I'm not that old, but can I just tell you that I feel like someone from a time machine. It's like everything changed and I don't remember when it did and don't think I voted for any of this and I'm just feeling all out of sorts.

My walk with God is good and I pray all the time, but I used to pray for patience with the kids or to not think bad thoughts about people or gossip. Now, I have to pray for Denny and Bailey's safety and school shootings and homeless people and war and now a murder and I just don't know what to think sometimes.

I question murder. Pastor Perry says that murder isn't God's plan, but we have to have the strength to go on. And I realize that the world's not ending with this, but it just jars you right out of any comfort zone you might have. Murder is what you see when you watch cable or the news from Jackson. You understand there's murder in the capital. There are too many people and not enough room, but that's not *here*. Romania barely has enough people to be called a town. If it weren't for the highway, I don't think we'd even have a red light. Nobody pays attention to it half the time anyway. And, it's not like there's an abundance of sites to see. No wonder the kids drive in circles around the Sonic on the weekend. I guess there's really nothing else to do. I mean the town only runs from the high school to Tawnette's north to south and from Hoblain's Funeral Home to the Sonic east to west. It's only got about 3,000 people and I'm counting dogs and slow squirrels. Of course, if anyone did decide to do anything wrong, you can rest assured that it would be all over town the next morning. Secrets just aren't safe around here. If anyone got away with anything, I'd be surprised. That's what's got me all confused. You'd think that somebody would know who killed Dr. Boddy or at least that the person who did it would *know* they'd get caught. I mean, if you can't accidentally squirt mayonnaise in your best friend's face on 'Ham Yumbo Day' in the cafeteria at school (this happened to Denny) and your Mother not get several phone calls within an hour (courtesy of the cafeteria monitor, the janitor and the school secretary), how can you kill somebody and not get caught? It just doesn't make sense. *Somebody* always knows *something*, you know? This shouldn't be too hard a case to solve. Of course, Sheriff Stiles isn't going to go out of his way to do anything except hire every cousin of his he can find. Nepotism could be his middle name. Come to think of it, with the way things are around these parts, it might actually *be* his middle name. I've never asked.

It doesn't matter if I don't know how it happened or think it shouldn't have happened or have faith in the police department, Dr. Boddy is still dead and Finney will need consoling…I think. She sounded upset, but it was more irritated than anything. I don't know, maybe she's in shock. I know Finney and as much as she puts on, she's a good person deep in her soul. Deep, *deep* down in her soul.

Chapter 6

Barreling through the door like a child about to tattle, a red-faced Finney panted for a glass of tea. The redness didn't worry me so much as her cheeks are always a strange shade of scarlet due to more than a passing acquaintance with Mary Kay cosmetics and, well, either rosacia or high blood pressure- I've always been too uncomfortable to ask. I handed her a tall glass and she gulped it down and panted, "He would have to pick May of all months to die."

"Well, Finney, I don't think he had it penciled in his planner," I said taking her empty glass and refilling it from my favorite crystal pitcher. It's Mikasa; an anniversary gift from Denny last year. He shouldn't have spent so much on it, but he's just like his Daddy; generous to a fault. I love it. When I use it I feel all fancy like Martha Stewart. You know, before the prison thing. I like to pretend it was just a really bad made-for-TV-movie, except *not* starring Cybill Shepherd. Don't get me wrong, I like her and all, but I don't think she had enough panache to make me believe it was really Martha. Martha's not southern but I just adore her. Still sweating profusely and downing the second glass, she added dramatically, "It must be 700 degrees outside! I hope no one expects me to wear black to the funeral. I'll die from heatstroke!"

Mother, who had been sitting unnoticed (by Finney), suddenly harrumphed at this breach of etiquette; you know, speaking flippantly about death.

Ignoring Mother's stare, I suggested that Finney could wear white like they do in Asia. Denny told me that once.

Laughing heartily, she said, "Do you know what I'd look like in all white?"

"Fog," muttered Mother as she made her way out of the kitchen.

"You don't seem to be too upset about Noe being gone," I said, once we were alone.

"I don't think I really believe it yet. You don't know how it is living with an arty type; always so high strung and *very* theatrical. I guess I think he's playing a practical joke to teach me a lesson about appreciating him or poetry or art or something."

"I don't think I know *any* dramatic people, could you describe them to me," I said sarcastically, looking at the very personification of drama.

"I'm not *that* dramatic," she huffed. "Anyway, I guess I should have listened when he said he felt like someone was following him. I thought he was joking."

"Well, it is hard to believe."

"He told me he'd leave a clue, if he was killed."

"He really thought he would be killed?"

"I guess so," she frowned. "You see why I didn't believe him? It just sounds so improbable."

"Well, I just don't know what to say."

"I guess I should have listened, but who'd want to kill him? I mean, his poetry's not *that* bad."

"If he thought he was going to be killed, why didn't he call the police?"

"He said he talked to Harlon Stiles, but they just laughed at him and told him he'd been watching too much TV."

"That's kind of rude, but I can see their point, I guess," I said. "Did he say what kind of clue he'd leave? Did the police find anything?"

"I don't know," she shrugged. "I just didn't believe him. I'll call Harlon Stiles tomorrow," she said, her words tumbling over each other.

"Have the police said anything?" I asked.

"They ruled it an accident, pending an investigation."

"Even though he told them it would happen?"

"Yep. Sheriff Stiles said they're on the case."

I laughed ruefully, "Then again, these are the same cops who supposedly trailed an escapee from the county jail twelve miles into the woods when he was really hiding across the street, behind the National Guard Armory with a broken leg."

"According to the police report, he supposedly fell and hit the back of his head on the desk in his office, but they found him sitting upright in his chair. I realize Noey was obsessive-compulsive, but I find it hard to believe he cleaned up after he died."

"Were there any witnesses?"

"The only other person on campus was Two-Dan."

"Two-Dan Walker?"

"Do you know somebody else named Two-Dan?" she said, rather sarcastically, I thought.

"How'd he get to the school?"

She replied, "Noey had started taking him at night just to have an extra body around. Made him feel safer, he said. Ironic isn't it?"

"Well, has Two-Dan said anything? I mean anything that made sense?"

"I saw him when I got to the school. Sheriff Stiles said they found him out by the concession stand repeating 'macaroni'."

"I thought we only sold frito pies and pig lips."

"I know I shouldn't laugh."

"Have they questioned him at all?"

"I'm sure they weren't very nice or patient. Good manners aren't Harlon Stiles' strong suit. You know how hard he is on Gentry and that's his son. Jimbo Jakes told me that he just kept repeating 'macaroni' and sat there, looking sad."

"Macaroni, huh?"

"Yeah, weird isn't it?"

"How'd Jimbo know?"

"He's a cop now. First week on the job."

"Land sakes. He's about the dimmest bulb in the chandelier, bless his heart."

"True, true. I guess that's why they had him interview Two-Dan; you know kindred spirits and all that."

Mother reentered the kitchen and asked, "What's a Two-Dan?"

"That's just an old guy from around town," I answered. "His Mother, bless her poor ignorant soul, named him after two of her friends, Dan Mills and Dan Fulbright. Instead of just naming him Dan, she named him Dan-Dan."

"Who ever heard tell o'such?" Mother scoffed. "Well, to tell the truth, I remember when I was a girl, there was a woman name of Stone, Rosetta Stone, and she had twin girls and named them Dilly Gee and Gilly Dee. So, I guess I *have* heard tell o'such," she laughed.

Turning to Finney, who was laughing, she said, "You don't seem to be too upset about losing your just-about-to-be-ex-husband or whatever it was you called him."

"Well, it's not like he was my first love," she responded. Seeing Mother's arched eyebrows, she quickly added, "Don't get me wrong, I did care for him but he *is* husband number four and we *were* legally separated."

"*Four* husbands?" Mother asked incredulous.

"When you say it like that it sounds bad," Finney answered defensively. "I married the first time for love, the second time for money, the third time out of loneliness and the fourth time, well; I can only plead temporary insanity."

"Temporary?" Mother smirked.

Finney retorted, "Don't you have small children to scare somewhere?"

Mother aimed her response at me; "I'm going outside to sit on the porch with my wonderful son-in-law who would never allow his hippie friends to talk to *his* poor helpless Mother any old way."

Finney's cell phone rang and she walked onto the porch to take the call.

"If you're helpless, then I'm the Queen of Sheba," I said.

"Smart talk will get you in trouble Your Highness," she said before stalking after Finney through the side door to the porch where Mac always sits. The fieldstone patio gives a magnificent view of everything down our road all the way to town. If you shield the sun from your eyes, you can see the football field at the high school. Well, as long as Cornbread Avery isn't burning something in his backyard. If I had my druthers, he'd just build a big old dome over that land, so we wouldn't have to look at them. I don't want to be mean, but the Avery's idea of yard work is working in the yard on whatever happens to be there, whether it's a boat motor or an old tractor. At least they don't have that conglomeration of concrete I-don't-know-what-alls the Whipstarts have in their front yard. They live over near Finney and, I promise you, it looks like Disney had a garage sale. Fawns, turtles, elves, squirrels, everything you can imagine, including matching 3 foot tall ceramic mountain goats wearing overalls super-glued to the porch, by the steps. Of course, they don't really match anymore as one is now missing its head, thanks to their Great Uncle Rooney who has a 'familiarity' with alcohol and various other substances I won't mention, because decent people just don't. Oh, I know I shouldn't be gossiping like this, but I'm on edge about Dr. Boddy and hopefully you can see it in your heart to not pass judgment.

Finney came back into the family room and I asked, "Are you sure you're all right? How're you holdin' up?"

"Oh, I'll be fine. I just need one thing," Finney said, looking as sincere as I've ever seen her and placing her hand on my arm.

"Name it darlin'."

"Help me find the killer."

I was stunned. This was unexpected. I sputtered, "Just because I have a bicycle and a cardigan doesn't mean I'm Jessica Fletcher. What do I know about solving a murder?"

"You don't have a bicycle," Finney responded.

"Work with me here, I'm having a moment."

"I need your help, Cady. Jimbo Jakes is too stupid and Harlon Stiles is too lazy to find out anything. They're already saying it was an accident."

"Well, mercy, Finney, what can I do? The only things I've ever solved are logic puzzles."

"Those are the skills I need. That was Blythandi Jeskin, Noey's teaching assistant, on the phone. She said she found something she thought might be a clue."

Chapter 7

Well what do you know – Denny told me that the original definition of 'clue' was a ball of thread. That's why you unravel a mystery. Well, Finney's ball of thread was a doozy that I had no idea how we could use. All she had for us to go on was 7777, typed on Dr. Boddy's computer screen. Ms. Jeskin, but not the police, noticed this. When she brought it to their attention, they brushed it away, saying that he probably hit his head or something on the 7 key and it stuck. Blythandi didn't agree, so she called Finney.

When she arrived, I was automatically suspicious of her. She was inappropriately dressed unless she was headed to a field to hoe cotton. She was tall, slender and athletic looking. I'm assuming she was wearing a sports bra, because there just wasn't much there, if you know what I'm saying. Her clothing was oversized on bottom and undersized on top and her baseball cap (!) was, well, worn correctly, if a bit jaunty, but its presence caused me great concern. Do these young women not have suitable clothes? She looked like a boy who had stopped in the middle of changing clothes and walked right out the door. Maybe she had. Let's hope so.

Finney shared, "The only connection I can think of is that he loved trivia. He used to say, 'My mind is filled with useless information.' Or maybe I said that. Anyway, those sevens must mean something."

"This murder was brought to you by the number 7," Blythandi said, seemingly oblivious to Finney's emotional state or maybe she was in shock, too.

Finney laughed sadly.

"You know, it's all right to cry," I said patting her hand.

"Humans are the only animals that cry. Did you know that?" Blythandi asked.

"I guess I never thought about it."

"Noey told me that once," Finney said. "He was always telling me crazy stuff like that. What'd he call it? Minuta…Minute Maid…"

"Minutiae," Blythandi answered.

"Yeah, that's it," I said.

"He was smart," Blythandi said. "That's why I liked him. I didn't really care for his poetry, but I liked that he didn't like stuff that you're *supposed* to like."

I asked, 'What do you mean, *supposed* to like?"

"You know how it is. If a girl doesn't want to be a beauty queen or bake a cake or wear a dress, then she's, to quote my mother, 'bound for a life of torture and unhappiness.'" She rolled her eyes. Her Mother Blythe Ann Jeskin, the school district's Nutritionist, is one of those old guard Southern mothers who doesn't take kindly to change and I really can't blame her. If we could produce a new generation of Donna Reed's, we'd be happy. Honestly, we'd settle for a few 'That Girl's' if push came to shove. Of course, we know this new generation of young women can win a Nobel Prizes, cure cancer or run for President. We're not unreasonable; we want them to follow their dreams. We just would rather they follow them in a sweater set and handbags that match their shoes. Is that so wrong?

"Oh, it's not like that anymore, is it?" Finney asked.

"Why don't you come down to the school one day and see how popular I am and all I do is wear baggy jeans and ball caps. Its nuts, if you ask me."

"Now, Blythandi, I know for a fact other girls wear jeans to school. My Denny just graduated three years ago and his girlfriends or friendgirls or whatever wore jeans," I said.

She waved her hands in surrender, "Okay, maybe I'm exaggerating to make my point. It's just that if you're different, then you're just weird. It's not like I've been ostracized or anything. I mean, Sonic's too small a place to ignore somebody, but people just look at you like you're a freak. I can't wait to go to college."

"Well, not everyone can be the center of attention," Finney said.

"Oh, I know that. I guess it doesn't help that I make fun of those wannabe beauty queens, like the Dufresne triplets," Blythandi smiled.

"Are they in your grade," I asked.

"Oh, yes they are and I tell you I give them fits. That Cherry Dee sure thinks she's something special. Maybe I bring it on myself."

"Noey always did have a soft spot for troublemakers," Finney smiled, winking at Blythandi. "He was always making fun of this town, but I think he secretly liked it."

"It sure seemed to me that he hated it here," I said.

Blythandi answered, "I agree with Miss Finney. I think he secretly liked it here, too. I think he felt like he was on a mission. It was up to him to 'help them'. And I guess I was his sidekick." She smiled again.

Finney asked, "About this clue you found; what do you think it means?"

"I don't know really," she answered. "It seems kind of cryptic, but I still think it's more than just an accident. I realize Sheriff Stiles is in charge, but he's not too bright if you ask me."

"Oh, we're with you on that," I said. Maybe I could look past her ball cap, but that poor excuse for a blouse, on the other hand, had to go. Why advertise what's not there.

"It could mean anything. Too bad Two-Dan can't tell us. I'll just bet he would know. You know Dr. Boddy had him at the school all the time."

"How'd you know that," Finney asked.

"Mama always makes me go with her when she's working late on the menus or inventory or whatever. She's says I can't be trusted alone at home."

"Who else would know Dr. Boddy was at school so late?" I asked.

"I guess whoever drove past. His office faces the road. It wouldn't be hard to tell someone was there, considering everyone else runs for the woods at the stroke of 3:30."

"I guess you're right," I frowned.

"And you can't miss that orange car of his," Blythandi added.

Finney smiled, "Yeah. I always liked Big Citrus. That's what I called it."

"Well, I'm gone," Blythandi said. Turning to Finney she added, "I'm real sorry, Miss Finney. Mama said to tell you that you're in her prayers. If I think of anything, I'll call you."

Finney smiled and said, "Thanks honey. I know Dr. Boddy thought of you fondly. And thanks for your help."

I added, "Tell your Mama we said 'Hey!'."

"I will."

After she left, I turned to Finney and said, "My goodness, do they all dress like that?"

"Like what?"

"Like boys or farm hands."

"Don't be mean. Kids dress differently these days, Cady. Cut her some slack."

Indignant, I replied, "I don't doubt that, but she was most definitely inappropriately attired to visit someone's home."

"Well, Cady, she was in a hurry with evidence about my husband's murder."

Not to be deterred, I continued, "And I hope and pray that she is actually on an athletic team, otherwise, that cap has to go. We need to invite her over for a makeover."

"Look, Cady, I need you to focus on the task at hand."

"What task?"

"Solving the murder."

"You're right, let's get this solved and get her into some Claiborne. I'm sure that's what your Noe would have wanted."

"I don't think Noey cared how Blythandi dressed."

"You know what I mean."

"Knowing him, he'd probably want me to compose some iambic-pentametered ode to the futility of life and under-utilized genius. However, as I'm not even sure I understand what I just said, I think I'll stick to the detecting," she finished, looking tired.

"Sister," Mother said reentering the kitchen, "I didn't know y'all had a yard man."

"What?" I asked confused.

"Well, honey, I just saw the cutest little yard man walk right down the driveway. Well I guess he was a yard man, although he did have a car or any equipment."

"No, that was Dr. Boddy's teaching assistant. *She*'s not a yard man."

"She! Are you sure that's a she? My lands, that girl could do with a trip to Ann Taylor Loft," Mother added. "I just don't know anymore; boys and girls looking alike, both wearing caps and earrings and I don't know what all." She just stood there shaking her head.

I assume she remembered why she had come back into the room because she suddenly jumped and said, "Oh, and I just saw the most darlin' lady on the TV. I think she was a librarian. Aren't you looking for one of those?"

"Yes, we are! Who is it?" Finney and I asked, excitedly as we are both on the Library Board and have been desperately looking for a replacement since our current librarian-on-administrative-leave, Randa Holley, was arrested for kidnapping and assault. Poor dear had apparently reached her breaking point with patrons returning books stained with peanut butter, jelly, chocolate, greasy fingerprints and whatnot. I won't go into the details, but suffice it to say; in the future little Jacoby Martin will make sure he doesn't eat French fries and read a book without a napkin. And seeing as how Randa had slapped his mother, Anne Claire, in front of about 20 patrons and Board members before taking Jacoby on a bookmobile ride he won't soon forget, we felt sure she'd be convicted. We definitely needed a replacement and librarians are not in abundant supply in a town this size.

"I think her name is Randa or something like that," Mother said brightly. "She looked darlin' on TV, although I think she might be Pennycost because that collar was almost as high as her hair. Well it wasn't *that* tall, so maybe she's backslidden."

"Mother, she is going to trial for assault and kidnapping. She's the one we're trying to replace."

"Well I was just trying to help. You need a little more beauty behind the counter of that library of yours. A few less pounds wouldn't hurt them either. What was the criteria, first come, first served?"

"Are you talking about the volunteers?" Finney asked. "They work for free. I don't care what they look like."

"Obviously they don't either," Mother responded. "I just think you shouldn't hire somebody to replace her until she actually goes to jail."

"Mother, we all saw it happen. We were there. She'll be convicted," I tried to explain.

"I just don't think you should judge people. I know I raised you better than that," she stated, which effectively ended the conversation as Finney and I both stared at her open-mouthed.

Chapter 8

The next morning, since I had to think of a way to help Finney solve the murder, I decided I needed no distractions. I have always been amazed that I can concentrate on any number of things while I cook, so I banished Mac to the porch with strict instructions to stay put until I brought him some peanut butter fudge – what I had decided to make – and he readily agreed. I hadn't slept a wink the night before and still couldn't for the life of me decide what all those sevens meant. Oh, I had plenty of ideas, but none that made a bit of sense. I mean, how do you start an investigation? I needed some help. Too bad, Tom Selleck wasn't out in the back weeding my garden. That would be useful.

Mother, having been rebuffed from my kitchen as well, declared I was unworthy of her company anyway and decided to retire to the porch with Mac. She just wanted an audience for her stories, which I normally enjoy; however, I couldn't risk losing my focus or I'd be no help to Finney. Once I commit to something I'm dedicated to the cause, even if it seems insane. I needed an epiphany, something to do with 7s. The opposing sides of dice always equal seven, but the nearest casinos are down in Biloxi. Besides, that's almost an hour away even if you take the shortcut down through Bogalusa and we almost never go there anymore. I figured the killer could have come from the Coast, I mean they are just overrun with the mob. At least that's what that book "Mississippi Mud" said. Well, if that's where the killer is then, I say let sleeping dogs lie. No sense in having everyone killed. Plus, Dr. Boddy didn't gamble that I knew of and there isn't anything up this way to interest a mobster. I mean, we don't even have a jewelry store.

Finney said she needed my logic skills to help her. If the solution were in an acrostic, we'd be good to go. Maybe I need to buy a bicycle. I need to call Denny and see if he's coming in this weekend. I need to call Bailey and just talk. She's dating that Millard boy who's in the Navy and I'm just not sure he's the one although Bailey sure seems to think so.

I need to check on Miss Hildy; she's down in her back again. I'll never understand why these women in their 70s and 80s feel the need to exercise. I think they've misinterpreted the meaning of 'Sweatin' to the Oldies'. As long as I'm making a list I need to lose 10 pounds. On that note, I need to stop making fudge. Well, that's enough crazy talk.

Judges is the seventh book of the Bible. I wonder what the seventh word of the seventh verse of the seventh chapter of the seventh book of the Bible would be. Hmm…'by'. Well that was a dead end. Maybe I should use NIV instead of KJV. I don't think Dr. Boddy was very religious. I had a sneaking suspicion he was agnostic, although he was certainly Baptist enough to come to the Fifth-Sunday dinners on the ground. All that good Baptist food could turn Madelyn Murray O'Hare into a choir member; I'm here to tell you. For all I know, the 7s could mean the seventh King of Tuscany. Whoever that is; wherever that is. France? Italy, maybe?

As I stirred the butter, peanut butter and marshmallow cream to a boil, I kept trying to focus on the 7s, but kept getting sidetracked. I think I might have ADD, but I doubt it's anything that exotic. I'm probably just getting old.

What on earth makes Finney think we can solve a murder? How do you even do that? Denny's best friend Victoria is in school at Ole Miss to be a forensic scientist like on NCIS, but I don't even know her phone number anymore; not since she moved away to college. And my educational background doesn't cover anything like that. I have three years of Early Childhood Development. I can make a child confess to shooting spitballs but I can't coax a murder confession out of a random person. I think Finney's going overboard on this, but what can I do? I think she's using this to cope. I'll bet she feels guilty about not believing Dr. Boddy when he said he was being followed. But, can you blame her? You have to admit, it's a bit far-fetched. I mean this is Romania for pity's sake.

We don't have murders here. Hunting accidents? Yes. Car wrecks? Of course. The occasional thresher-related fatality? Sure. But not outright murder. Sheriff Stiles doesn't have any experience with this stuff. The most he ever does is write tickets for drunk drivers on tractors. I just don't have much faith in his abilities or those of our illustrious police force.

And goodness knows that my family is not in the detecting business. My Daddy was a farmer as was his Daddy. Mac's from a family of sharecroppers and carpenters. Denny and Bailey are the first people in our family that look like they'll finish college. I dropped out after three years to get married and just never went back. I've thought about it, but I guess I think I'm too old.

I heard a new voice outside and decided to practice my investigating techniques. Feeling not a bit like Matlock, I strode to the front door and saw Finney coming up the walk.

"No matter how many times I see you do that, it's still a sight," smiled Finney. It's true. Mac does cause many double takes, as he is a 6'2", 240 lb. man who crochets. The older ladies don't find it as amusing as Finney, seeing as how he has been the Franklinton Fair Craft Show Champion nine years running.

Mac just laughed, his meaty fingers furiously looping and pulling the thread that would become what has turned into a treasured wedding gift around here. We get invited to every wedding in these parts as every bride or bride's mother wants one of Mac's afghans.

"Cornbread shoot atcha?" he asked Finney.

Remember, I told you our road is book-ended by the Avery brothers, Catfish (to the north) and Cornbread (to the south). Would that make my house the cole slaw? They have a tendency to get agitated and fire at passersby, much to the dismay of their mother Belva Jean. These are some hateful boys; I'm here to tell you.

"No," Finney answered, "he must've been busy out back."

"Prob'ly drunk," laughed Mac.

"Wouldn't you drink if you were his age and found out your mother was pregnant?" Finney asked.

"Belva Jean Avery is pregnant?" I gasped.

"Who in the sam hill are you talking about?" Mother interrupted.

"Cornbread Avery. He's the one who lives down there," I answered, pointing toward the end of our road.

"The one with all the junk in the yard? Who'd name their child something like that?" asked Mother.

"Belva Jean," laughed Finney. "His real name is Levester."

Mother shook her head and said, "Well, I guess Cornbread's easier to spell."

Sniffing the air, Finney turned to me and asked, "Do I smell peanut butter fudge?"

"That's right," I replied, "it's cooling."

"Well, while we're waiting, Mac who's the afghan for?"

"Ask Cady," he answered. "Some Flossy June from town; I can't remember."

"You hush," I said to Mac. To Finney, I answered, "It's for Little Marsha Fairfield."

"Little!" Mac laughed. "That girl could haul grain to market!"

"That's so mean," I admonished. "She's a sweet girl and can sing like a bird."

"Yeah," he said, still laughing, "a big, fat bird."

"You," I said, giving him *the* look, "get no fudge."

Finney interrupted, "She does have a pretty voice, as long as you don't look at her."

"Are y'all talkin' about that girl from the church? She could eat a corncob through a fence with those teeth, bless her heart," Mother said. "Who'd marry her? Did he lose a bet?"

"Ross Hastert," I answered. "He's a nice boy from a good family."

Finney asked, "Those oil people from Liberty? They've got money."

"Well, good for her. I hope she'll be happy."

Truth be told I had been afraid Marsha would never get married. First off, she's in her early 40s and still lives at home. She's "little' Marsha because her mother is also named Marsha and you can't just call a girl Marsha Jr. She teaches at the high school with Dr. Boddy and is so sweet and so smart. She has the most beautiful singing voice. And it's not like she's always been alone; she dated the Youth Minister at Searcy Baptist for a long time. He actually proposed and she accepted but he took a job in Georgia before they got married and she wouldn't leave her Mama and Daddy. I'm glad her fiancé has money. You can fall in love with anybody; they might as well have a little money. I've had no money and I've had some money and money's better. I don't care what anybody says, it just makes things easier.

Finney said, "I always had a soft spot for her newly rich self."

Mac added, "Well, she's got several soft spots to choose from."

Mother and Finney laughed

"Y'all are just awful," I said. "I shouldn't reward bad behavior, but come inside. The fudge should be ready."

As we left the porch Mac whispered to Finney (or what he considers whispering, which is actually only lowering his voice a few octaves), "Bring me some fudge. I'm hungry as a hostage. Cady's trying to starve me to death." They exchanged a wink.

Stepping back onto the porch, I said to Mac, "You've already had cookies."

He tried to look innocent. I smiled, "Men with beards have no secrets. You've got crumbs in your chrome." That's what he calls the gray in his otherwise flame-red beard. Are you surprised he's a redhead? McIntyre doesn't exactly bring to mind tortillas.

"As nice a fella as I am," he pouted.

I reentered the house to the strains of his favorite ditty, "I don't know, but I've been told, a green grasshopper has a red..."

"You hush that trash talk," Mother interrupted.

That I find his little songs amusing is an admitted weakness.

Already Finney was hovering around the table, eyeing the plate of my most famous dessert. They say it's not a holiday without my fudge. Well today was no holiday but it was a special occasion nonetheless.

Mother came inside and sat eyeing Finney who was still eyeing the fudge.

"I'm gonna wash my hands. Y'all sit down and I'll get some plates and coffee," I said.

"I guess I shouldn't eat this," Finney commented, "its not healthy. Surprisingly, Noey didn't eat sweets anymore."

"Really?" I asked, disbelieving.

"Yeah, he had gotten on this health kick," she explained. "You know yogurt, rice cakes, and deep breaths."

"Are you sure," I asked. "He had doughnuts every time I saw him."

"No, those were Two-Dan's," Finney answered.

Mother interrupted, "Then why was he so fat? I saw his picture in the paper today."

Finney responded icily, "Some of us are genetically predetermined to be heavy." To me she asked, "Can I have a piece?"

Mother shot back, "Bull feathers! You're only genetically predetermined to be tacky. Don't eat it all."

Ignoring Mother, Finney turned to me and said, "You want to ride into town with me. Trudy Jasper gave me a gift certificate to the I Love You Shoppe instead of flowers for Noey's funeral."

"That's so tacky!" I exclaimed.

"She wasn't raised right," Finney and Mother answered in unison.

Finney, apparently not as unnerved as Mother at having agreed, continued, "Have you made a decision about helping me?"

Mother asked, "Helping you do what?"

"Cady's helping me solve Noey's murder."

Mother laughed, "Well if that's not like the blind leading the stupid."

"Mother, I will have you know that we (motioning to myself and Finney) are fully capable of solving this or any other murder," I said with more confidence than I felt.

Finney grinned at Mother, baring all her teeth.

"Nice teeth," Mother smirked. "What color is that, taupe?"

"At least they're all mine," Finney retorted.

"I have all my teeth, thank you."

"The ones in you purse don't count."

"That does it!" Mother said and abruptly stood and swiped the plate of fudge. She sidestepped Finney as easily as Fred and/or Ginger and laughed as she went out the door.

"Well, I guess that's that," I smiled.

"I think your first murder should be an easy one to solve, so I'm going to confess now," Finney declared.

"Confess what?" I asked, flustered. Surely she hadn't killed Noe.

"I killed your Mother," Finney said, heading toward the porch.

Finney returned with several pieces of the rescued fudge and sat back down. She seemed distracted and didn't actually take a bite. I was worried about her.

"You alright?" I asked.

"I guess. I mean, it's not like I hated him. We were in love once – for a long time really. I'm gonna miss him."

"I know, darlin'", I said, patting her hand.

"I know that I don't normally get upset about stuff, but I don't know what I'm gonna do."

"But you were planning on moving once the divorce was final, weren't you?" I asked.

"Well, yeah, but I guess it hadn't really sunk in – I'm truly alone."

"You are never alone, Finney," I said. "You've got us and you've got God."

"You I know about. God, I'm not so sure. I'm not a Christian."

"God cares about you even if you're not a Christian and all you have to do is believe in him and invite him into your heart and it's a done deal."

"It's that simple?" she asked.

"It's that simple," I said, walking over to give her a hug.

"You know I'm just having a hard time processing everything," she said. "I'm gonna need a lot of support."

"Always, Finney. You know you are my best friend – every crazed inch of you."

Finally starting to smile, she said, "And I'm gonna need some more of that fudge."

"Guaranteed. Unless it's raining. It's hard to make fudge when it bad weather."

"Then you can switch to pie."

"Done deal," I laughed. She really is me best friend despite our many differences. And it hurts me to see her hurting so much, but we'll get through this. I have enough faith for the both of us. And enough dessert recipes. We should be set.

Chapter 9

"Has every woman in Bogue Chitto County read the Southern Belle Primer?" Finney blurted as soon as I answered the phone.

"Well I have, if that helps." I said, smiling to myself. I sometimes forget Finney's not from here, bless her heart.

"I've got six green bean casseroles and four Jell-O salads sitting on my buffet," she whined. "When's the last time you've eaten those not directly related to a funeral?"

"You mean, *besides* Thanksgiving, Christmas, Easter and fifth Sunday potlucks?" I answered, trying not to laugh.

"I don't want the truth, I want to complain."

"Oh, sorry, I didn't get the script for this conversation," I said. "Is this why you called?"

"No, well, yes, well, sorta. My reason is two-fold," she stammered. "First, I need you and Mac to come help me eat this stuff and second, I need you to help me get ready for the Rue invasion."

"Rue? As in street?" I asked confused. Since when did Finney start speaking French? We're not *that* close to New Orleans.

"No, as in rue the day. Noey's sister is on her way here; although I *would* like to run her down in the street."

"Oh, she can't be that bad."

"She made Noey seem like a big ol' teddy bear."

"My stars. Okay, I'll be there in a minute."

"Don't forget to bring Mac, so he'll eat," Finney reminded me. "And I guess you can bring..."

"Don't worry, Mother went with Deltrenda Walley to the Senior Center to play Mexican Train and Chicken Foot. She'll be gone all afternoon."

"That sounds like voodoo," Finney laughed.

"It's dominoes, Finney. We don't have voodoo here. This is not New Orleans. We'll see you in a few minutes."

After we arrived, I fixed Mac a plate and sent him to the den to watch TV while Finney and I talked about the arrival of (according to Finney) Dr. Boddy's only living relative – Ruetrisha. According to Finney she was an unmarried, spiteful food service manager for the 'Walls of Jericho' religious compound somewhere in West Texas.

"She cannot be as bad as you say. Everyone has a good quality of some sort."

"Oh, Pollyanna, spare me!" scoffed Finney.

"I resent that..."

Finney interrupted, "Resent it all you want. The fact remains, you *are* overly optimistic."

"And that's a bad thing?"

"It's just not realistic, Cady. Trust me this woman has no redeemable qualities, unless you give her credit for matching the handle of her cattle-prod to her shoes."

"I'm not sure I want to be here for this."

"You have no choice. You're my best friend and cannot desert me in my hour of need. Well, it's more of a weekend in need. But you promised to do anything to help."

"Darn me and my good intentions," I pouted.

"It'll be fine; she's only here to make sure she gets her part of the insurance money. Well, that and to irritate me. She normally only stays long enough for me to start thinking of creative ways to kill her, then she's off to do whatever it is she does in that place in Texas."

"What exactly is that place? A cult?"

"I don't know really. It might be, but you can never tell. They can't be too choosy about membership seeing as how they took in Ruetrisha and let her cook. And you thought Jim Jones' cool-aid was bad."

"Finney Boddy, that is not in the least bit funny," I said. "I watched that movie. It was so sad. People are hurting so much and so desperate for something that they'll kill themselves for what they think is the truth. You need to start coming to church with me more!"

The phone rang and Finney dove for it. "Sorry Cady, important call."

Suddenly she frowned and asked, "You're where? Describe the area. *Besides* lots of trees and fences. Do you see a water tower? Is it on your right or left? Do you see a church? Okay, go straight ahead and take the first road to the right. It's called Forsythe Lowery Loop. Because *every* road has somebody's name. It's because of 9-1-1. No, not 9/11. Can I explain it to you once you get here? Oh, good grief. Once you turn right, we're the third house on the left, red brick with a barn behind it. No, there won't be chickens in the yard! Well, my God, it's not the 'Dukes of Hazzard'! FINE! Good-bye!"

"I'll take a guess and say that was Ruetrisha herself."

"Tell me more about church, Cady," she pleaded. "Jesus is gonna have to intervene or I'm gonna hurt her! Her highness got lost among all the 'bugs and dirt'!"

"Bugs and dirt? It's not like West Texas is some lush oasis, for pity's sake!"

"She's a moron; I gave explicit instructions. It's not like it's hard to find and she's been here before. We're not even a half-mile from the highway. And you're right, she's from West Texas. At least *we* have trees."

I felt guilty, talking about her before I even met her, so I said, "Well if you're not familiar with the area..."

"Cady! I need you to be on your meanest behavior. You'll have to be to survive. Trust me she is a minion of the dark forces."

"But, I'm not a mean person," I protested.

"Remember last year when Marcetta Steeple talked about your new haircut and then helped vote down your idea for a fundraiser?"

"Oh, I can't stand that woman!"

"There ya go, keep that in mind."

"And her with her big ol' Pennycost hair all fluffed up to glory," I growled. "And that *was* a good idea..."

You know that phrase, "Politicians make strange bedfellows"? Well, a couple of years ago, it was an election year and I thought that it would be fun to have all the candidates for all the state offices some to the library and sit on a bed and answer questions. I thought it would generate some interest in the elections, which are so important but not very interesting. At the very least it would have made for a great picture for the Romania Free Press, our local paper. Jalinda Combs, the editor, thought it was a great idea, too, but what I call the 'old lady brigade' led by Marcetta voted it down, saying it "didn't send the right signals, having a bed in the library".

I guess I had stopped talking because Finney said, "Cady, sweetie, focus please. Because I swear, anymore rude behavior from Ruetrisha and she'll be a gone pecan."

Finney seemed to enjoy having the home field advantage. She was acting as if she were preparing for tactical maneuvers. Standing on her front porch she strode between the columns like Scarlett O'Hara awaiting the next wave of Yankee invaders, but without the turnip or the torn dress. I thought she was overreacting until into her driveway pulled the largest Crown Victoria I've ever seen commandeered by *the* most Republican-looking woman I've ever run across. Not that it's a bad thing to be Republican; it's just not necessarily good. It's like when you take a bite of day-old meatloaf. One bite may not be bad, but more than that will haunt you for days.

Ruetrisha alighted from her carriage and strode toward us with a withering look plastered on her immaculately colored face. As she neared, she remarked snidely, "Finnella, how kind of you to invite me to your… little…homestead."

Turning to me, she stated, "You're Cady." As if I wasn't aware myself.

"I didn't invite you Ruetrisha, the lawyers did. Darn that Jerelyn Fortenberry."

"It's good to see you're as charming as ever," she quipped.

My first reaction was that of the meatloaf, but I smiled my smile that didn't involve my eyes and followed them into the kitchen. Misinterpreting my I'm-only-smiling-because-I-was-raised-right smile to be that of a compatriot or an idiot, Ruetrisha turned to me, sniffed the air and frowned, "The stench of iniquity pervades the air around here, don't you agree?"

Over her shoulder Finney snapped, "It didn't until about three minutes ago."

Once we were inside, Finney offered Ruetrisha something to eat, only to be rebuffed in favor of a tour of her home. Finney protested that she had been there before, but Ruetrisha insisted, saying she so enjoyed the "amusing décor". I really couldn't argue with her, although in Finney's defense her home reflected her personality which, I feel, is perfectly acceptable. I had grown used to her color schemes. Although I would never fully appreciate the apple green cabinets in her kitchen, her bedroom in Neapolitan was absolutely scrumptious. The chocolate browns, deep pinks and rich creams made you want to stay forever…and eat. Her cream silk chaise just screamed for someone to lounge while being fanned and/or fed grapes by some eunuch (is that the right word?) from ancient somewhere.

Anyway, Rue, as I will now refer to her because I'm tired of typing her full name, seemed only to want to ridicule Finney and I was having none of that. In the face of poor treatment of my friends, I can lose my religion, so to speak

"So, Rue, can I call you Rue?" I interrupted a dialogue about her disdain for sectional sofas, "What religion is your place in Texas?"

"Religion?" she asked, perplexed.

"Yeah, you know, are you Moonies or Mormons or did you just make something up?"

With one hand clutched to her chest and the other raised toward, I'm assuming, heaven, Rue snarled, "How dare you refer to 'Walls of Jericho' in such a glib manner!"

"I'm simply asking what denomination you are," I continued, innocently. "Baptists and Methodists don't have compounds. How do you feel about David Koresh?"

"What's wrong with having a compound," she demanded.

"Well, unless you're a Kennedy or a cult, you don't really need one, now do you?"

"I will not stand for this Finnella!" she ranted as she spun toward the kitchen.

"Would you rather lie down?" laughed Finney.

"Finnella, if this is the treatment I can expect, then I shall find accommodations elsewhere! I'll see you at the funeral!" She stormed out of the house and through the garage as Finney yelled, "If I had known that I'd have tried harder on the phone."

Laughing, Finney turned to me, "You know that wasn't exactly Christian behavior."

"Eh, it was a judgment call," I said shrugging. "She shouldn't have been rude to you. That was totally uncalled for."

"You are such a good friend," she said, starting to tear up.

"Are you okay, honey?" I asked.

"Yeah, between Noey and then Rue and then you being so sweet, I'm just all emotional. If I start to sing 'Wind Beneath My Wings' slap me."

"Don't worry."

Chapter 10

Once I got Finney all squared away at her house, Mac and I left with enough leftovers to get us through a nuclear attack or at least the 4th of July. I had given Finney some suggestions of what to wear to the funeral from a book of Denny's I found in the bathroom called Stuff You Didn't Want to Know or somesuch.

I had to get home and get myself ready. Mac was easy; black suit, black boots, combed hair and *voila* - Johnny Cash meets Conway Twitty, just like the Good Lord intended. I on the other hand had to find just the right balance. I'm not vain, mind you, but you do need to always look your best and black tends to wash me out, so I have to add a touch more makeup. Then you start to worry, is it too much? Do I look like Tammy Faye? You know that Bartell girl from out near Arvid Springs? Lord she can wear some makeup. She always looked like she ran into the side of an adobe house, you know like out in Arizona. Except that orange color never went below her chin, leaving her neck looking as shiny and pale as an uncooked turkey. It was downright off-putting. I'd never look that bad, but it doesn't take much for people to start talking about you. Of course, Mother will set me straight if something's not right, believe me.

Once Mother had approved of everyone's outfits, we piled in her car and then had to get out because Mother forgot her White Shoulders. We went back into the house to get it and when we came out Goober was in the back seat. I guess he wanted to go. Then it was back in and out for breath mints and water and tissues. Then Mother decided she smelled 'dog' in her car, so we had to get into my van. Well, it took near about twenty minutes. I'm usually so organized and have everything in place, but I guess we were all out of sorts. Plus, I had decided to take the little black pocketbook Denny got me for my birthday. It's so tiny and pretty and not good for one darn thing except to look at, like one of those girls on the *Price Is Right*. Do they really need people to point to the door of the microwave, like I don't know where it is? Don't get me wrong, it's a great job, if you can get it, but it hasn't been the same since Janice and Holly left.

We drove up to the funeral home, Thornton's not Hoblain's – it's nicer. Mac, Mother and I were about to enter the foyer when we were startled by a high pitched wail that sounded so pitiful it brought tears to my eyes.

"Sounds like a panther with its tail on fire," Mac said, looking around.

"My word," I cried, "Either Finney's killing Rue or she's more upset than she let on!"

"Who's Rue?" Mother asked.

"She's Dr. Boddy's sister. That woman from earlier at Finney's house?"

"The Moonie?"

"No. Well, I'm not sure. She never would say."

"Figures. You know those people from West Texas. Crazy from the heat is what they are."

Mother pushed me inside, "Well get on, Sister. Go find out what's what."

I flung open the doors of the viewing room and was greeted by the sight of the 82 year-old identical twins, Lolly and Bitsy Keene, sprawled across the casket crying in truly heart-wrenching sobs. I had no idea they, or anyone for that matter, were so attached to Dr. Boddy.

I approached them with the apprehension of an inexperienced animal wrangler. Passionate Southern women can be frightening, especially if you interrupt such a public display. Actually *true* Southern women are brought up understanding the connection between propriety and emotion in public. These are the Keene sisters, however (the irony of their names is lost on no one) and although they have lived here for a number of years, their mother's people are from Florida, which is most certainly *not* a southern state. We like to think of it as North Puerto Rico. Anyway, I felt it was my duty to quiet the ruckus.

"I'll give you a green bean casserole if you stab them in the throat," Finney suddenly whispered in my ear.

"I first thought you were killing Rue," I whispered back.

"I'd never do that here. Too many witnesses, although this dress is a dark color. It wouldn't show the blood stains as much."

"Finney Boddy, you ought to be ashamed!"

"I will be if you don't shut those women up. I've got peanut brittle if you do."

I smiled and made my way to the front of the church and leaned over to (I think) Lolly. I could never tell them apart until they smiled. Lolly had a small crack in one of her teeth. I don't know the name of that particular tooth. It's near the middle, front. Let's just say that if her teeth were the Supremes, she's chipped Cindy Birdsong.

I stepped toward one of them and said, "Come with me darlin'; it looks like you need a shoulder to cry on."

"Oh, Cady!" she wailed, "Isn't it awful! To be taken in the prime of life!"

"I know sweetie, but you have to calm down, you'll just upset everyone else. Get…uh…your sister and let's sit down. Dr. Boddy wouldn't want all this fuss."

She stared at me like I was crazy and asked, "What does the opinion of that obnoxious man have to do with anything?"

"He's just a big donkey fool," said Bitsy. She had finally smiled.

"It's his funeral," I answered.

"What?" they said in unison, which is unnerving.

"This is Dr. Boddy's funeral. Didn't you know that?"

"This isn't Billie Shannon Foster's funeral?"

"Lord, no, honey. She's here. In the back row, with the big yellow hat."

"Well, my mercy, you'd think she'd at least dress nice for her own funeral. That hat's awful," Lolly mused.

"Looks like a big taxi on her head," Bitsy chimed in.

"She's not dead, Lolly," I repeated.

"Well, that's no excuse for that hat."

After the service, we decided to go back to my house, with or without Rue. Well, it was going to be without, if I had anything to say about it. I know you're supposed to love everyone, but I just don't think I can. After the way Rue acted before during and after the service, well I know what righteous anger feels like, do you hear me? She managed to insult everyone at the funeral home and I'm just not sure where she got the idea that she was anything special. I guess she must be the right hand to whoever or whatever runs 'Walls of Jericho' place, because let me tell you she has a misguided sense of herself.

Out of courtesy to Finney, we invited everyone, including Rue to join us in finishing off the abundance of food that is so readily offered to families in crisis. That's a Southern response to an emergency/tragedy – pray and eat.

Thankfully, Rue declined our invitation and chose to retreat to the "charming B&B" she found in Columbia, a larger town about twelve miles west of Romania. She wouldn't subject herself to this 'backwater hamlet' any further until the meeting with the attorneys in a few days.

"My lands, that woman was some character," Mother said about Rue once we were in the car. "She makes that Marcetta Steeple woman seem downright pleasant."

When we got back to the house, Mother started laying out the food and wanted to know if I could help her fold our napkins into swans.

"Why so formal, Mother?" I asked.

"Catherine Dyanne, someone has passed on and we can't make things nice for everybody? I know I raised you better than that," Mother admonished.

"But, I thought you didn't particularly care for Finney," I whispered.

"Sister, while I think your friend is seriously in need of charm school, a makeover and a psychological evaluation, personal feelings never trump etiquette. You know that. Now help me get everything ready and after we eat, we can play Rook," she smiled.

"Good idea," I smiled back, "maybe that'll keep her mind occupied."

"Exactly," she replied. She walked into the family room and asked Finney if she wanted anything to drink.

Finney, looking a bit wary, answered that she'd love some tea.

"Fine, then, you go on into the living room while I get the good china," Mother told her coming back into the kitchen.

Finney came to the doorway and frantically waved me over.

"Oh my God, Cady, I'm so sorry."

"Sorry about what?" I asked.

"Either your Mother has gone crazy or she's plotting to kill me," she said hurriedly.

I laughed, "Finney, honey, she's not insane and she's not going to kill you. She's simply Southern and old habits die hard. If we let our feelings rule our manners, there wouldn't be any Yankees living down here, now would there?"

No sooner than we had Finney situated in the living room, everyone showed up. Apparently it was a slow day in Romania because I mean *everybody* was here, including Velberta Stiles who doesn't even like Finney, but she sure likes potluck. I laughed looking at all the green bean casseroles and Jell-O salads. Finney rolled her eyes and headed straight for the platter of brisket that Hubert and Deltrenda Walley had brought. People were clustering in groups after paying their respects to Finney who did her level best to look the part of a tragic widow. She had taken my advice of wearing purple. I read in that book that's what they wore to funerals in Turkey and if anyone questioned it (and nobody with any class would say something to her face) she could just say that it was in honor of Dr. Boddy's fascination with the Middle East. That'd confuse them so much, they might even leave. I was hoping against hope that Marcetta Steeple would say something. Now listen to me being all tacky. I'm sorry. I just don't particularly care for Marcetta.

After the Mennonites sang several songs, including Mother's favorite 'Amazing Grace', people started to drift onto the porch to leave. The Mennonites always sang at funerals for those they respected. Dr. Boddy's position as an educator afforded him that designation. It was most assuredly not because they liked him. Dr. Boddy could have made Will Rogers amend his famous saying. But let's not speak ill of the deceased.

It was getting late and we were all tired. I was glad it was all over – the funeral that is. We still had the mystery to solve, but we could postpone that for another day.

I walked into the living room, thinking everyone had gone home when I spotted the Keene Sisters and Belva Jean Avery in the corner having the most animated conversation. I walked up and they turned to me smiling brightly.

"Hi, Cady," beamed Bitsy. "Wasn't this a lovely funeral?"

"I'm glad you enjoyed it," I smiled tiredly.

"The best part was when Billie Shannon got some three bean salad on her hat," Lolly laughed.

"How did that happen?" I wondered.

"Well, I put it there, silly. It was the most awful hat," she giggled.

"It was almost as ugly as her shoes," tittered Bitsy.

"Her shoes? What about her husband?" whooped Lolly.

I had to laugh. It seems that Billie Shannon is not the most popular person in Romania.

"Y'all are awful," Belva Jean interrupted.

"We're sorry, Miss Belva, we'll stop. We don't want to upset the baby," I said.

"Belva Jean, is this true?" Lolly was ecstatic.

"Yes, it is," she sighed. I guessed this was not the happiest news she had heard since the last tragedy her family had faced. There were so many that you could just pick a year and there'd be something awful tied to her family including the births of her two sons, Catfish and Cornbread.

"Well, we think it's wonderful," Bitsy chimed in. "You'll finally be a grandmother."

"Ms. Bitsy, Ms. Belva Jean's having the baby."

"What?" Bitsy and Lolly said in unison again.

"It's her baby, not her grandbaby."

"Well, that's just silly. She's too old to have a baby," Lolly said.

"Don't tell me," I said.

Turning to Belva Jean, Bitsy repeated, "You're too old to have a baby. It's just silly."

With that Belva Jean stormed out of the house, leaving all three of us surprised; her flailing right arm slapping the doorframe on the way out.

"Cady McIntyre!" Lolly fumed, "You go apologize to her right now."

"What? I didn't say anything," I stammered.

"Well don't tell tales on top of it," Bitsy chastised. "I think it's time you went home."

"Yes," Lolly added, "Good day, young lady."

"Uh…" I started. It would do no good to argue, so I left the living room and hoped they'd leave before supper. Sure enough, they walked out about 20 minutes later, wished Finney 'Happy Birthday', thanked me for a wonderful party and walked out the door.

Chapter 11

After Mother and Mac had thoroughly beaten Finney and me at Rook (I swear, that woman can 'shoot the moon' with no trumps and still win), we decided to take a breather and work on our theories about the murder. Can you believe I'm using that word in casual conversation now?

Doing what I do when I have a project, I decided we needed a list. You always need a list. If I do something that's not on my list, I add it to the list, just so I can mark it off. Is that strange? Deciding she was to be the secretary of this little undertaking Finney took the pen and paper from me and said, "Let's take the simplest route first. What's something simple with four 7s?"

"Well, four times seven is 28, but that could be anything."

"Maybe we shouldn't multiply. You know there's a bunch of 'seven' stuff."

"Like what?" Finney asked.

"Like the seven seas, for one."

"What has that got to do with anything?"

"Well, I don't know. I'm just trying to think."

Finney sighed, "Maybe there isn't any significance. Maybe Harlon Stiles is right and it was just an accident."

"Did you just hear what you said? Harlon Stiles can't possibly be right. We'll just have to try and solve it, even if we make fools of ourselves."

"But what could it mean? 28?"

"You know what? The Cotton Bale is on 28 Boughton Street," I said, excitedly.

"It can't be that easy."

"You don't know – it might be. What other ideas have we had?"

"If that's it, why didn't he just type 28 instead of 7777?"

"That would be your husband, not mine"

"Well, it does seem like something that would amuse Noey to no end. He loved making things difficult".

"Do you think there could be a clue at the Cotton Bale?"

"I don't think the clues in my kitchen. It couldn't hurt to go find out."

"Now?" Finney asked, "Shouldn't we wait 'til dark or something?"

"Are we going to go undercover? Like on TV?"

"I guess so. If the police aren't going to help, then we have to do something."

"I guess you're right," I responded, "Although, I don't know how much we can do. We don't know anything about stakeouts."

"Well, let's just go and see what we see. Mercy usually closes at 9:00 so she can have her nightly fling," Finney said.

Mercy Coffman is the proprietress of the Cotton Bale, Romania's one eating establishment if you don't count the Sonic, Tawnette's Wagon Wheel or the Deli at the Piggly Wiggly. Her husband Cletus works offshore and she carries on like wanton street trash, oblivious to the fact that everyone suspects, except, apparently, Cletus. I mean, if I know about it, then you know it's gone through the gossip mill.

"I'll come over about 10:00. Noey'll be in bed...Oh, Cady!" she whispered.

"C'mere darlin'. It's okay," I said, as I pulled her into a hug.

"I act so tough, but I do miss him. I thought about killing him on several occasions, but I didn't *really* want him dead."

"Well, I'm here for you," I promised.

She looked at me and started to sing, "Did you ever know that you're my hero?"

I interrupted her and smiled, "Do you want to lie down? You're overwrought and I don't want to have to slap you."

She laughed, "No, I'll be fine. I never realized my singing was that bad."

"I'll reserve my comments."

We decided to take my mini-van because Finney's car is conspicuous from anywhere. Denny says you can see it from outer space and I'm inclined to agree. I made Finney drive, though, because I was just plain nervous. Being the oldest girl in my family, I've been spied on, just never the other way around. I just don't know if I'm cut out for this. But a promise is a promise.

Noticing Finney had put on the blinker to turn right, I assumed she meant to park in front of the Farmer's Co-op.

"No, don't park there," I said. "We'll be in plain sight of the police station. Park behind the Methodist Church and we'll walk."

"I don't want to walk," she pouted. "This is an investigation, not a workout."

"Detective work requires you to be on your feet."

"Not Ironsides. He always sat down."

"He was crippled, Finney."

"I want a wheelchair."

"How about I break your legs and then we'll get you a wheelchair?" I threatened.

"Okay, okay," Finney replied, waving her hands in surrender, "behind the Methodist Church. Are you on hormones?"

"I'll ignore that."

We crept to the rear of the Cotton Bale using our take on stealth which was me on tiptoe (I don't know why) and Finney cursing quietly under her ragged breath. As we neared the kitchen, we heard moaning.

"We were right!" I stammered, trying to remain quiet, "someone's in there trying to kill Mercy!"

"What do we do?" Finney whispered.

"I don't know! If we rush in there, we'll be killed too!"

"No cream," a voice moaned.

"You're right," I responded, "Don't scream. That'll only draw attention."

"What? Who're you talking to?" asked Finney.

"You! You said not to scream. I was agreeing with you."

"I didn't say anything."

"Use the filling, coconut," said the breathless voice.

"Good idea. Go with your feelings. I think we should try to call the police. Use your cell phone to call Jimbo. And I am not a nut."

"Number one, are you high? Number two I forgot my cell phone in the car."

"How rude."

"Well, I'm sorry, I'm not used to having one yet."

"Not that, you know good and well that I don't use drugs. Are you delirious from the walk?"

"You're the one hearing voices. Are the dogs telling you to kill again?"

"Would you kindly stop talking? They'll hear us and Mercy won't be saved," I said.

Rising to peek into the window, Finney replied, "She doesn't need saving from the looks of it."

Joining her, I unfortunately saw more of Mercy than I ever wanted. She was *in flagrante delicto.* I'm not really sure what that means, but I know it's dirty. What was going on, well, decent people just don't discuss things like that. I *will* tell you I'm ashamed of Gentry Stiles and I will never eat at the Cotton Bale again. There are certain things you just don't do on a kitchen counter. Don't get me wrong, I'm ashamed of Mercy too, I'm just not as surprised. Gentry is the sheriff's son, named for his mother's people, and he desperately wanted to work in law enforcement. However, being that his IQ was somewhere in the neighborhood of a really good golf score, he had been turned down by everyone, including the National Guard. Still his desire remained evident in his wardrobe. Everyday he wore BDUs, which stands for Battle Dress Uniform- its camouflage. Didn't I mention Bailey's fiancé, Toby, is going into the military? That's why she's in school in Charleston, at the College of Charleston. Toby is studying Engineering at the Citadel.

Of course, as is usual, Gentry took it one step too far by painting his truck camouflage too. And, no, he didn't pass the written exam to get a license. In small towns, driving a car and having a license are not necessarily synonymous. I remember when Jemma Beth wrecked Daddy's new truck when she was only eleven.

Finney, who was apparently not as appalled as I, just laughed and said, "Gentry, you little hound. Military or not, he's got some pretty good maneuvers."

"Eeew! Let's go," I whined. "That's a rumor I'd rather not have confirmed."

We ducked back down and I motioned for Finney to leave. I had just about had enough of the whole situation. As I'm not one to gossip much, I never needed to have this tidbit of information. Finney was a different story; she'll have a field day. Anyway, we still hadn't come any closer to solving the murder.

Finney interrupted my train of thought, "Cady! Let's go!"

Mercy and Gentry had stopped *delicto*ing and were moving toward the door.

"I gotta gun!" Gentry blurted out.

"Run!" I yelled and took off, with Finney hot on my heels. We made it back to the car in record time, without disturbing anyone, most especially Jimbo Jakes or any other member of our talented police force. I collapsed against Finney's bumper to catch my breath. Finney lay on the ground at my feet, gesturing feebly for me to lean toward her, as if she were breathing her last breath.

I leaned over and she whispered, "Must...hurt...you."

"Well," I said, after we made it back to my house, "that was a wasted effort."

"*Au contraire mon* Cady. This is some of the best gossip I've heard. It's the only gossip I've seen," Finney laughed. "Now we've got a face to put with the activities, whip-creamed though it was."

"Stop! I can't take it. But, can you believe them? I'll never be able to look them in the eye again."

Finney laughed, "I, for one, will not be able to eat coconut cream pie again."

"Hush," I begged, "I don't want to think about it."

Mother, having entered the kitchen where we were sitting said, "Don't you dare hush, I want to hear what happened."

As Finney filled her in on the scoop, I made coffee and sliced some of the sock-it-to-me cake that Mother had brought back from the WMU luncheon at Javista Farnham's. Those Golden Girls were onto something; there's nothing like sweets to calm the nerves.

"Isn't Gentry Stiles that slow one who always wears camouflage?" Mother asked.

Finney smiled, "Normally, yes, but tonight he was just wearing a big smile."

"Again with the nakedness. What's in the water around here?"

Finney and Mother laughed like two old chums. This odd turn of personalities was not uncommon in my family but only came about in the face of really juicy gossip or when confronting a shared enemy, like DeeDee Smandon. Mind you she's not an enemy in the traditional sense of the word, but giving her a wide berth was never a bad idea.

Chapter 12

Before we got sidetracked and maybe overlooked some clues in the 'neighborhood', I decided I needed to go on a fact-finding mission with Mother. Finney had an appointment with Jerelyn Fortenberry about the will. She'd be having a rough enough day.

I decided to start at unofficial historian Malvina Jamison's house as it's the last house on the edge of town on Highway 37 (which is called Boughton Street within the city limits) going towards the high school and she'd also be privy to the latest goings-on. I figured that she might have seen or heard something the night that Dr. Boddy was killed. Finney and I had decided that it must have been somebody who knew Dr. Boddy taught at the school and would be there at night. Miss Malvina's driveway was about ten feet from the road leading to the school, called, appropriately enough High School Road.

Since the 9-1-1 emergency system came to small towns, every road had to be named. Those who are tasked with this more often than not, named the road after who had been there the longest or any historical marker, real or imagined. That's why it's not unusual to have people living on a road named after them. A perfect example is Miss Malvina who we're about to visit. She lives on Roland Jamison Road (her late husband), even though she's the only house and it's actually her driveway. Of course, there's names like Old Stoner Church Way, where the church isn't anymore or Fulton Massacre Road, where the massacre didn't actually happen, but I guess that's beside the point. As there is no Pitty nor is there a Pat, I don't know why they named our road Pittypat Lane, but, there it is and what can I do?

Mother said we should walk, seeing as how we had eaten a year's worth of sweets and casseroles in the last few days and didn't want to gain any weight. When I informed her that it was almost 6 miles between our house and Ms. Malvina's, she suddenly decided that the humidity would wreak havoc on our hair and that a ride in air-conditioned comfort would be just fine.

When we pulled in the driveway of her place I marveled at the sight of all the flowers she had growing which made the house seem larger than it was. Like many homes in small towns, it had started out as a shotgun house, but as families and incomes grew, so did the many additions. Although you couldn't really tell since they'd had vinyl siding installed in the last few years, I remembered the different stages of growth and could place events in my life to coincide with each addition.

Once we stopped the car, we noticed Ms. Malvina on the roof and got out of the car calling, "Ms. Malvina? Why're you on the roof? You could hurt yourself."

"It's that durn paperboy Dill Lumpkin. He doesn't even slow his truck down. Just roars past here going 80 miles and hour, driving with his knees and never even looks at the house," she recounted, climbing down the ladder. "At least I found it today. Some days I'm not so lucky. He's just, I don't know. If he wasn't older than me, I'd tear his behind up!"

"Why don't you call the paper and complain?" Mother asked.

"I guess I could, but then he'd just get fired and him and Elsie with all those grandkids living with them since Maureen and Bill got killed over in McComb. I can manage a few more climbs before I give out completely," she smiled. "Y'all come on in out of this heat."

"You don't have to ask me twice," Mother smiled.

"How long's Dill been delivering your paper? I thought he retired," Mother asked.

"He did," Malvina replied, stepping onto the porch, "but the railroad pension only pays so much and Maureen had six children. It's just not enough. Poor Elsie had to go back to work at the Cotton Bale until they get the money from the wreck."

"If they get it at all," Mother added. "Speaking of the Cotton Bale, have I got some news for you."

"Mother, now's not the time or the place for that. You know why we're here. Besides, how'd you know all that?"

"Well, Sister, it's not like I don't live here. You hear things. How do you think I know Malvina?"

"I thought you were just being polite. Where'd y'all meet?"

"Sister, who do you think goes to the Senior Center? Cheerleaders?" Mother laughed.

"Oh, well anyway, we didn't come here to gossip, we came for a specific reason," I held.

"Y'all have a seat and I'll get us something to drink," Malvina said, motioning to the kitchen table, which I assumed was the large object covered with knickknacks, potted plants, give a dog a bone. I'm just kidding, but honestly, could she have one more item in that room? Every square inch of her wall was covered with photos, drawings and one of those clocks where the cat's eyes and tail move back and forth. Her brown and white Formica countertops were lined with books and jars of preserves and, while it wasn't messy, it was *full.* I guess she can't let go of anything.

"Fine," said Mother, "business first, gossip second."

Ignoring her, I began, "Ms. Malvina we want to ask you a couple of questions, if that's all right."

"Sure, honey, ask away. I'll help you if I can."

"Well, we're trying to help Finney, you know Finney Boddy, solve her husband's murder."

"Murder!" Malvina gasped. "Harlon Stiles told me it was an accident. Told me right to my face!"

"Well, that's the official story," Mother agreed, "but Finney and Cady seem to think otherwise."

"Finney said Dr. Boddy was afraid that he was in danger," I said, defensively. "And we've found a few clues, but we're looking for anything you can remember about last Wednesday night."

"Murder," Malvina repeated, oblivious to what I had said, "right here in Romania. Well, I just don't know what to think." She had suddenly turned pale.

Taking her elbow, I guided her to a chair and asked, "You okay, Ms. Malvina? Have you seen anything suspicious at all?"

Robotically she asked, "Did y'all want something to drink? How about some lunch? No, it's too early for that. Are y'all hungry?"

Mother stood and walked toward the sink, "Malvina, you sit down, I'll get you some water."

Malvina continued, "I'm just stunned. Nobody's been murdered here since 19and74, when that girl was killed out by the lake. But she wasn't even from here. Just some girl, they said, from over Hattiesburg way. It's not the same as somebody you know."

"Was it drugs? There was a girl killed over in Laurel for drugs. Saw it on the news."

"Mother, that's now. She's talking about the 70s."

"Cady," Malvina interrupted, "I think she's right. It *was* drugs."

"Are you sure it was 1974?" I asked. "I don't remember that."

"Well, let's see," she said, closing her eyes and looking up as if searching a large invisible timeline. "I think it was '74. It was just before Helga Morgan died, but after Belva Jean married Clyde's boy Luther. Those two should've not got married. Well, married is fine, but they shouldn't've had any children. Those two boys have never been all there."

"I know," I added, "I couldn't believe they'd have another."

"Belva Jean Avery is pregnant?" Malvina gasped. "Land sakes, that woman's too old to have children! I thought she had her tubes tied?"

"Evidently not," Mother said, shaking her head. "I realize that people have the right to be happy, but there's a limit."

Malvina asked, "Isn't Belva Jean your age Cady?"

"Actually she's older than me by a few years, although she graduated the same year. I've been told she was supposed to have graduated in '65, but she kept failing English."

"Well," Malvina sighed, "I guess they wanted to hear the pitter patter of little feet again."

"Then they should get a little dog," Mother smirked.

"Rain," Malvina laughed, "you are something else."

I questioned, "How do they think this kid'll ever be normal?"

"Normal compared to who?" Malvina asked.

"She's right," Mother said, "I'm sure she thinks Coondog and Biscuit are just fine."

Laughing loudly, I said, "Their names are Catfish and Cornbread."

"Like there's a difference," she snapped. "What're they gonna name the new baby, Hushpuppy?"

"Mother, that's awful."

"Cady, you leave her alone. They are a strange bunch. I was talking to Belva Jean's mother, Hilma, last week at the Piggly Wiggly and she was just going on about Cornbread and how grand he was," Malvina laughed.

"Sounds like she's as stupid as Belva Jean," Mother commented.

"Where do you think Belva Jean got her ways? Her Daddy's all right, but her mama's never been all there. I guess I'll have to buy it something when it's born," Malvina mused.

Looking at me, Mother said diplomatically, "I suppose we will, too. It might as well be dressed cute if it's gonna be an idiot."

Turning to me Malvina asked, "Now tell me about what you were needin'?"

"Well, we want to know if you'd seen anything suspicious lately."

"Suspicious how?"

"You know, weird or out of the ordinary. Something just not right."

"Well," she started laughing, "Crespo Peterson came by the other week wanting to mow my yard, and between me you and the fence post, I swear he was wearing his wife's clothes."

"Ms. Malvina, you are making that up!"

"I most certainly am not. It said 'Hot Mama' in glitter on the front. I don't believe it was for a man. Leastways any man I'd want to know."

Mother interrupted, "Isn't he in that family that lives out by Junior Foster in all those trailers welded together? Must be twenty of 'em."

I looked at her.

"Okay, fine," she huffed, "it's not twenty, but it's more than a few."

"Well, that's neither here nor there," I said, "they're nice people."

Malvina harrumphed, "Fiddlesticks, Cady, you think everybody is nice. I don't like to speak ill of folks, but his family is trashy. I swear they'd eat an apple in the bathroom and throw the core in the tub."

"They look like they'd smoke in the shower," Mother added.

"Anyway," I said, trying to redirect the conversation, "why'd he ask if he could mow your yard? Doesn't Lobo Kitchens mow it?"

"Well, of course, he mows just about everybody's," she answered. "It was strange though, Crespo kept talking about seeing my house on his way back into town Wednesday night. Said he noticed my yard and would've stopped then, but said he didn't see any lights on. Kept asking me if I was home, which made me downright nervous."

"What was he trying to get at?" I wondered. "He knows you go to choir practice on Wednesday nights, doesn't he?"

Mother asked, "And how would he see your yard at night anyway?"

"You're right, Rain. And, I assumed he knew I would be a church normally," Malvina said, "'cause his mama sits right behind me, she sings tenor, but I missed last Wednesday as I had a headache somethin' fierce. I had all the lights off hoping it would go away, but I definitely heard his truck."

"How do you know it was his?" Mother asked.

"You know how loud those old pulpwood trucks are. They make all kinds of racket. I'd know it anywhere."

"Well, there are plenty of trucks around here like that," I countered.

"At night?" she replied, "I don't know anybody that drives a truck like that all the time."

"You may be right," I admitted. "Well, we'll get out of your hair, Ms. Malvina. Thanks for your help." I stood to leave.

Mother and Malvina stood and walked toward the door.

"Oh, here, honey, y'all take one of these philodendrons. I've got 'em comin' out my ears," she said, handing me a potted plant from the table. "If

I don't start getting rid of some of this stuff people are gonna start talkin' about me."

I accepted the offering, "Well, thank you, Miss Malvina. That's awfully sweet of you."

"My pleasure, Cady," she said, turning toward Mother. "Now, didn't you say you had some news about the Cotton Bale, Rain?" Malvina asked.

"Oh, I almost forgot. Cady and Finney saw Mercy and Gentry Stiles doing stuff you shouldn't so close to a hot stove."

"Or anywhere else," I added.

"Oh, Lord, y'all got to leave. I'm gonna get another headache with that picture in my head."

Chapter 13

Now I've been felt compelled to head somewhere quickly, and I've even taken to speeding a few times, but I have never seen anything move as fast or with as much determination as the rooster Mother and I saw running down the side of the highway on our way back from Miss Malvina's. I'm here to tell you that he was running for his life. And I'm not real sure if he was running toward or away from something, but wherever he was headed, he'd be there soon enough. Mother and I had a good laugh about it and decided maybe we should follow his lead and head for the hills.

We hadn't been home long when Mac decided to grill steaks for lunch. It sounded good to me, so I asked Mother to help me make all the trimmings, like potato salad and corn on the cob. I parked Mother in the kitchen watching everything that was boiling. I decided to set the table and had no sooner started toward the breakfast nook when Finney came barreling through the door madder than a wet hen. She had just finished the meeting with Jerelyn Fortenberry and Rue about Noe's will. I couldn't imagine what had her so angry, so I just sat waiting for the dam to break. Even though she stopped short for a second when she smelled Mac's steaks grilling, she was not to be deterred.

"Oooooh, I cannot stand that big-haired Jehovah's Witness!" she spat.

"Jerelyn's not a Jehovah's Witness is she?" I asked as I walked around the family room looking for the perfect spot for my new plant.

"Not her; Ruetrisha."

"Oh, I didn't know that's what she was."

"Well, she's something weird and that's the first one I thought of."

"So," I said, "I guess it didn't go well?"

"If my being left penniless is a good thing then, yes, it went very well."

I gasped, "He didn't leave you *anything*?"

"Oh, he left plenty...of crap. The insurance money has to be split with some poetry commune and Ruetrisha. However, I did get all his books and personal effects. Yay me."

"A poetry commune? Where is it?"

"At Cane's Bridge, if you can believe that. It's called something stupid like Water Whispers or something. I can't remember."

"I thought a water whisper was a lawn sprinkler?" Mother said as she sat down with us.

"Maybe it is, I don't know. It's all there...in my purse," she mumbled, pointing at the huge beach bag she always carried with her.

I pulled out the document from among the candy wrappers, cheap sunglasses and tissues. A full one-third of the money left after debts had been settled would go to the Lojac Piedmont Memorial Whisperers of the Mighty River Poetry Circle and Fruit Stand. I wonder what hippies do when they get money. How on earth did they have a commune in Romania and we not hear about it?

Seeming to read my mind, Mother asked, "I wonder what they'll do with the money?"

"Probably buy dope or save a tree or something stupid," Finney sighed.

I tried to look on the bright side. "At least you got $125,000 and all the bills are paid."

"Do you know how long that money will last? A couple of years tops. I'll have to get a job."

"Why don't you apply for that Library job?" Mother suggested. "You look like all those volunteers; they might make you their queen."

"You could Finney," I said. "Maybe we can suggest to everyone that since we're having such a hard time finding a replacement, we can appoint you interim Librarian on the stipulation that you go over to Hattiesburg and get your Library Science degree. Wouldn't that be great?"

"I don't know," Finney frowned.

"It's either that or work at The I Love You Shoppe," Mother said.

"Ugh, I'd rather be poor. You really think they'd go for it?"

"It'd have to go for a vote but I don't think Billie Shannon hates you that much and everyone else likes you. I'll call LeLe tomorrow and see if we can't call a special meeting of the board."

"Who's LeLe?" Mother asked.

"LeLe Highsmith-Boone. She's the President of the Library Board."

"So, what's wrong with her?" Mother asked.

"What do you mean?" I asked, confused.

"Well, one of you always has some comment."

Finney and I looked at each other and shrugged.

I answered, "I can't think of anything I don't like about LeLe. She's smart and organized and dresses real nice and has good hair. She runs the Nursing Program over at the Community College in Platt's Landing."

Finney laughed, "And that's all we really ask of people."

Mother shook her head, "I don't think y'all have ever said anything about her. Is she married?"

"Yeah, her husband, Bridge, is that retired marine who announces at the football games."

"Y'all like him, too?"

"Yeah, he's great. He's always telling a funny story," Finney said.

"Well there's a first time for everything. Maybe we should invite them for dinner. I need to meet some uncrazy people around here," Mother laughed.

"Maybe we will, but first things first," I said and picked up the phone.

When I got back to the family room, Finney was sitting with her eyes closed. When I walked in she looked up and said, "I thought I'd put my brain to good use so we can get this thing solved before I lose my free time."

"You think of anything?" I asked.

"Well, Mac's grilling got me thinking about the Fourth of July and now that I'm feeling patriotic, I think we can go with another seven I just thought of, Andrew Jackson, seventh President of these United States."

The idea sounded good to me because there was a spot west of town not far from the river called Jackson Springs, a kind of park, picnic, make-out area, or so I've been told. It could hold a clue to this mystery, seeing as how the Cotton Bale was a total disaster and I couldn't figure out if there was any significance to what Ms. Malvina had told us about Crespo Peterson. The only thing that seemed to be going our way was the chance to gossip and eat, as if we needed more of that in our lives.

Finney and Mother had been having a field day. Since there's not much going on in a town this size, gossip is a favored pastime; most especially if it's actually true.

LeLe agreed to call a special meeting. She said she'd contact everyone and to make sure Finney's resume looked good and there were copies to pass out. I guess LeLe was as ready for a replacement as we were. We *have* been looking for a good six months.

Mary Myra would of course be there laden with desserts. She is as devoted to the feeding of our members as she is to her odd color schemes and synthetics. Don't get me wrong, she's a nice enough woman, I don't particularly care for her style of dress. The last time we had a symposium at the library, she wore bronze espadrilles with a green and gold pantsuit. The only time it is appropriate to wear bronze, in my opinion, is if you come in third at the Olympics. I know that sounds hateful, but I think people should try harder to look their best. It's not like she can't afford better, her husband Dale is an attorney. I guess she gets it honestly; her mother is Elmyra.

Finney and I had planned a rendezvous for the next night just so we could use that word in casual conversation and not feel like we were putting on airs. Mother had refused to go on the grounds that she was much too precious a commodity to risk life and limb if there was to be an altercation with the 'bad guys'. I warned her again about the dangers of watching so much television, but she insisted she knew what she was talking about. She reminded me that although raising three girls (me, Jemma Beth and Nolee) had prepared her for anything, even battle if necessary, she was not going to 'get caught up in all that mess'. When I pressed the issue that we might need her, she simply waved me away, pointed to the picnic basket full of food she had packed as we planned an all-night stakeout if need be and said, "I helped." She had easily distanced herself from the proverbial trenches, but I guess that was a good thing as it's hard to hide when there's constant arguing and/or laughing, depending on her and Finney's moods. Either that or she was just sick of both of us and wanted some peace and quiet.

For this outing I had planned ahead and chosen a stylish all-black ensemble as I remembered black to be *de rigueur* for espionage. When Finney finally showed up, she was wearing yet another one of her dizzyingly colored wind suits. I'm used to her clothes but goodness knows this one would have caused vertigo in a lesser person.

"I feel like Baretta," she beamed.

"The only thing louder than that outfit would *be* a cockatoo. Does it have a dimmer switch?" Mother asked.

Finney answered, "You cannot upset me tonight." To me she asked, "Are we ready?"

"As ready as I'll ever be," I replied.

"That's a dubious comfort to say the least," Mother remarked, handing me the heavy-laden basket.

Finney and I left the house with a walk more confident than was necessary. I think I pulled something.

"I feel stupid. What're we trying to accomplish?" I asked, struggling to find a more comfortable position. "There's a reason you don't see this in the movies."

We were stationed in a low tree near the picnic area. I desperately tried to remember what exactly Finney had said to convince me to scale this tree. Could've been 'snakes'. We didn't know exactly what we were looking for, but we were determined to find something if it killed us. Of course, those were Finney's terms, not mine. I was determined to find something so we could go home.

"Relax," she said, "this makes perfect sense. Although, if I slip, I'll be a gone pecan."

"If this makes so much sense, why do I feel like I'm trapped in an episode of Patty Duke?"

"You'd have to be Patty."

"Why do *I* have to be Patty?" I groused.

"Cathy was much more cosmopolitan. Remember, she's been to Zanzibar and Barkley Square."

"You know," I huffed, "If I didn't have the sneaking suspicion you were insane, I'd take offense. Remind me what we're looking for."

"A roving band of sevens?" she asked, hopefully.

"Now wouldn't that be tidy."

"Ssh!" Finney suddenly hissed. "Someone's coming."

After several long hours, two vehicles had pulled into the area nearest the water, where it was almost too dark to see. I couldn't make out their tags, but the truck was a four-wheel drive Dodge and the car was a Nissan Sentra. It could be anybody; those types of vehicles are as plentiful as dogs around here. Even my Denny has a Sentra.

"Can you see who it is?" I whispered, as she had the better view. I could only tell it was two men. From my view, it seemed to be two men.

"I can't tell from here," Finney whispered back.

"Well, go look. I'm sick of being in this tree. My legs are numb and I don't want to lose my balance. A gone pecan I'd rather not be." Whatever had possessed me to wear black in late May in Mississippi is beyond me. All that 'it's not so much the heat as it's the humidity' nonsense didn't help the fact that my shirt was stuck to my back although it was almost midnight.

Jackson Springs is a nice area at the south end of town. It's where we have the Dairy Festival and the Harvest Festival. We also have a lot of class reunions and family reunions. We have the Ripley family reunion at our old home place in Louisiana – Alsatia, to be exact. I know you don't know where that is. Even people from Louisiana have never heard of it. It's halfway between Tallulah and Lake Providence. My first cousin on Daddy's side Bill Patrick Ripley bought the farm after Daddy died. Mother kept on living in the main house until Covaletta died. Bill Patrick's son Chip (Bill Patrick IV) lives in the house now, with his new wife and their precious little baby. He's just started working with his Daddy. He went to Henderson University in Arkansas and got his Agri-Business degree and now helps run Ripley Farms which is about 8,000 acres of soy beans and rice. It covers a good portion of Northeast Louisiana. Bill Patrick and his family are pillars of the community, which makes me laugh sometimes when I remember how he was growing up. He's so successful now and that family could be on a magazine cover. Between him and his wife Sandra and Chip and their daughter Macy, they've got enough pretty to share with another family and still be attractive. If I'm lying, I'm dying. Macy works in fashion in New York City. She's the assistant for somebody named Zac Posen. I don't know who that is, but Denny said it's "major" and that celebrities wear his clothes to the Oscars and everything, so that's exciting. I hope he's not the one that did that weird dress for that girl who laid an egg. Remember, that? I don't know how I got off on that tangent. I guess I miss my family and am looking forward to the reunion in July.

Finney had slithered, surprisingly graceful, down the tree and silently approached the truck as both people had gotten in. She was almost to the door when the horn honked and Finney abruptly turned and ran back grabbing my foot as she went by.

"Come on!" she frantically whispered, "we've got to go!"

"What happened?" I asked as I made my way down the tree and ran after her. "What'd you see? A clue? What were they doing in that truck?"

"Let's go!" she said forcibly.

"Why did they honk? Did they see you?"

"I don't think so. Get in the car!" Finney yelled.

"Are we in danger?" I yelled back. So much for undercover work.

"Look, Andy Griffith said that the first person you see after an owl hoots is your beloved."

"What are you talking about?"

"Well, I just heard an owl and you're not my type. Get in!"

Chapter 14

We settled into a booth at Tawnette's Wagon Wheel. Since its Romania's only 24-hour restaurant, we didn't have much of a choice. The truck stop, which housed Tawnette's, was unusually busy. Well, I guess it was. I'd only been there a couple of times for Sunday lunch, and I haven't been anywhere at this time of the night since college, so this could actually be normal. Although I was full from the picnic Mother had packed, I was in need of some animal-fat induced confidence. Our trip to Jackson Springs, along with the trips to the Cotton Bale and Malvina's had accomplished little. The only thing that had changed was Finney's behavior. I couldn't get anything out of her.

"Finney," I pleaded, "for the umpteenth time, what did you see out there? Something spooked you."

"I think they may have seen me."

"Who?" I asked.

"I don't know. I couldn't see them. That's what frightens me."

"Well, it's neither here nor there."

"I disagree. My Great Aunt Verlisa used to say..."

"You don't have a Great Aunt Verlisa," I interrupted.

"Says you. My Great Aunt Verlisa always said, if you're gonna get caught doing something, you might as well know who caught you. And I don't, so let's order."

Well, I guess that's that. I didn't really have any idea what I wanted to eat or even whether I wanted to eat, but Marthy Stewart, no relation, had appeared at our table questioning our patronage 'at this hour', so I ordered a Lead Foot Special just to keep her busy and avoid more questions.

Ruby Mac, however, was not to be deterred. Ignoring her other customers, she sauntered over and smirked, "Whatchall doin' out so late?"

"Oh, we couldn't sleep," Finney lied, "so we decided to come eat some of your wonderful food."

"Is that so?" scoffed Ruby Mac. "Cady, you know I saw Denny in here earlier tonight, with Jimbo Jakes. What's he been up to?"

"Denny? Are you sure? He's supposed to be at school in Columbus, uh, you know he goes to the W," I stammered, regretting the way I said it as soon as it came out of my mouth. I'm proud he goes to the W. It's one of the best schools in the South and Denny just loves it there. But some people think it's weird and they'll judge my sweet boy. Anything to talk about somebody. His Daddy even thought it was an odd choice. Then he decided that maybe he'll find a wife there. I don't know though. Denny's never been one to date. He's much to busy.

"He didn't tell you he was in town? Hmmm? And I didn't know he went to MSCW. Ain't that a woman's school?" Ruby Mac sneered. MSCW is the old name for the school – Mississippi State College for Women. Even though it changed to MUW in 1974, old habits die hard I suppose.

Finney jumped in, "His school's called Mississippi UNIVERSITY for Women now and it's the best one around and he's on a full scholarship. Plus, it's been co-ed for more than twenty years." Go Finney! She's so protective of Denny.

"Maybe so," Ruby Mac said, frowning. "Y'all's food'll be ready in a little bit."

"Ooh, I can't stand her," whispered Finney when Ruby Mac left. "She's just trying to get you all wound up. Ignore her."

"You know I don't listen to a thing that woman says," I tried to smile. 'Everybody knows she's just a gossip." And it would be all over town tomorrow. How Finney and I ate at the truck stop well past midnight and Denny sneaking around town not letting his mama know he's home from his 'woman school'. And what on earth is he doing in town? He didn't call to tell me and he's good about calling. It's just strange. I didn't even know he and Jimbo were that good of friends. Well, I'll talk to him in the morning.

When Marthy brought our food and reminded us not to listen to a word Ruby Mac said (I knew she be gossiping) we decided to at least try to think of new seven ideas while we ate.

"Okay, you start," Finney began between spoonfuls of cheese grits.

"Well, let's see, I already thought of the opposing sides of dice always equal seven but I ruled that out since Biloxi's so far away."

"There's seven days in a week."

"Seven swans-a-swimming."

"Seven dwarves."

"Seven Brides for Seven Brothers."

"Seven Sister Schools."

After awhile of this back and forth, we still hadn't gotten anywhere.

"Aagh!" Finney groaned. "This is pointless. It doesn't make any sense."

I replied, "Not unless he was killed by a cartoon, Christmas or the State of Maine."

"The state of Maine?" Finney asked.

"Haven't you ever read Wendy Wasserstein? Denny gave me a book last year. Never mind, I'll explain later, I'm too tired."

"I'm with you. Let's try to sleep it off."

We paid the bill to a decidedly smug Ruby Mac and left for Finney's house so we wouldn't disturb anyone at mine.

Once we arrived at her house, however, we found ourselves still too keyed up to sleep. We decided, since we were awake, we would brainstorm until closer to normal breakfast time and then we'd go to my house and confer with Mother, or collapse, whichever came first.

"Can you think of *anything* else that has a seven in it?" I asked, trying to unravel that darn clue – persnickety thing that it's become.

"Let's see, there's the seven deadly sins."

"What *are* those?" I wondered aloud. "I remember pride, greed, sloth and envy."

"Hmm…there's gluttony, anger and, oh yeah, my personal favorite, lust!" Finney exclaimed.

I tried to muster a reproachful look, but instead said, "Well, maybe."

"Maybe nothing. It *is* my favorite."

"Finney, I am not talking about that. I meant maybe to it being a clue. Stay with me here."

"There's a seven-mile bridge in Florida."

"Too far away," I said, opening my eyes, "and how do you know that?" I was impressed.

"I'm reading the encyclopedia."

"Oh, okay. What about the Seven Year's War?"

"You mean the Austro-Prussian War?"

"Sure, why not," I smiled.

"Here's something about a Seven Day's Battle from the Civil War."

"Really?" I asked, "I've never heard of that."

"Yeah, it was in the summer of 1862. Uh, the South thwarted the North's attempt to capture Richmond, Virginia. That was the capital of the Confederacy."

"Thwarted?" I laughed.

"Hey, I'm quoting, okay?" Finney said, looking offended or just tired; I couldn't tell.

"Interesting as it is, it's completely useless."

"Look, I'm all sevened out," Finney answered, exhausted. "Maybe there's a book around here?" She got up to survey the odd collection of literature that practically littered her den, which was not necessarily a bad thing as it covered most of the burnt umber walls and brown carpet. She had taken the advice to 'paint a wall in some small room a color you're almost afraid of' a bit too far. The room retained the ability to make me uncomfortable and not just because it reminded me of that horrible bridesmaid's dress I had to wear to Eva Fay Lancaster's wedding back in '79. That's why I was keeping my eyes shut.

Keeping my eyes closed, I asked, "What about the Seven Wonders of the World?"

"What are they anyway?"

"Gracious Finney, it's been years. Let's see, there's the pyramids of Giza, the Colossus of Rhodes and the Hanging Gardens of Babylon. Hmmm, oh and the Statue of Zeus at Olympus. I can't remember any more. Look it up."

"Okay, but I know there's a book with a seven in the title around here somewhere. Here it is! Seven Interpretive Essays on Peruvian Reality by Mariategui!" she exclaimed triumphantly.

"My heavens, Finney, if that's a clue, I give up," I sighed.

"Nah, you're right. That's a bit too obscure even for Noey. Let's get back to the encyclopedia. Here we go. Oh, you were right. The ones you said plus three I've never heard of. I was gonna say the Leaning Tower of Pisa, but it's not here."

"I think these were the wonders of the ancient world," I commented.

"Here goes, the Temple of Artemis at Ephesus, Pharos of Alexandria and the mausoleum at Halicarnassus." Before I could open my mouth or eyes, she added, "Don't ask, I'm just reading what's here."

We sat staring at each other until, oddly enough, seven o'clock, when we decided we had wasted enough time and surely someone would be awake at my house. Mac gets up early every morning – he thinks the sun won't rise unless he's on the porch. Once there, we would recover and agree on a new plan with Mother's input. So far, our plan was most definitely not coming together. Maybe seeing Denny would relax us and help us think. Maybe

Denny would have some ideas, he's always been so smart. My precious boy. I still can't figure out why he didn't tell me he was coming home. I'm sure it's nothing – he's not one for secrets.

When we entered the kitchen, we were surprised to find Two-Dan eating at the table.

Mother turned and looked at us disapprovingly, "Y'all look like you've been rode hard and put up wet. What happened?"

"I'm too tired to talk," I answered feebly, while Finney just headed for the couch in the family room.

My gaze questioned Two-Dan's presence and Mother answered my silent query, "Well, he came to the door yelling 'macaroni'. I figured he was hungry. What was I supposed to do?"

"You should have let Denny drive him home," I answered.

"Denny? Sister, you *are* tired. Denny's not here, he's at school."

"What? Oh, yeah," I said. Denny's not home? Where on earth could he be and why would he be hiding from us? Maybe Ruby Mac just made a mistake? But she's known Denny his whole life; she'd recognize him. Well, I'll talk to him later.

I turned wearily and said, "I'm taking a shower. Then I'll drive Two-Dan home when I'm through."

Finney groaned, "I think I'll take one too, so I can be pretty for our next adventure."

"Darlin'," Mother smiled, "we don't have that kind of water."

Had she been conscious, I'm sure Finney would have said something.

"Sister, you get some sleep," Mother replied. "I'll take him home and have Mac ride with me, just in case. You know how people like to talk. And we can stop by the Piggly Wiggly on the way back and pick up something for a late lunch or early supper, depending on how long y'all sleep. How about some stuffed tomatoes with apples and pecans?"

"You'd better get something with meat for Mac," I whispered.

"Tuna *is* meat."

"Not to Mac. He'll need a pork chop or something."

"Well, then I'll just send him to the Sonic for his supper."

"Perfect, Mother. Thank you."

"Any time, Sister. Now go to sleep."

Chapter 15

After Mother and Mac returned from taking Two-Dan home and Finney and I had awakened from our nap, we decided to relax on the porch. The whole incident had Mother on a roll about crazy people in the family.

"It's like they said on Designing Women, 'In a Southern family, you don't ask if there's a crazy person, you ask which side of the family they're on. Now your Great Aunt Ida Ruth was always a bit off her beam, bless her heart. She was a precious woman, but she just saw things a little different. She died when Denny was three; the same year Jemma Beth had Madison. Jemma Beth's my middle daughter; she lives over near Tyler, Texas. Well, Ida Ruth didn't have the sense God gave a goose. She had three sons and named them all John, after her Daddy."

"All of them? You're kidding, right?" Finney asked.

"No, she's not," I sighed, "It's true."

Mother was not to be sidetracked. "Called one Johnny, one Jacky and one, Lord only knows why, Bobo."

"You are making that up," Finney laughed.

"I don't have to make it up, honey. But she did have her brand of logic. She said it was so people wouldn't know their monogrammed shirts were hand-me-downs."

"I don't believe that," Finney said, still laughing.

"Well, whether you believe it or not, it's true. Now, Bobo was the odd one of that bunch and that's sayin' a lot. He married a woman name of Coleen. She had spent time in the county jail for beatin' up a state trooper or some such. She would've gone to prison, but the man was too embarrassed to testify in court, which he should've been."

I interrupted, "In his defense, Coleen is about 5'12" and weighs around 300 or so pounds."

"And she drives a Subaru Brat, if you can believe that," Denny added walking in the door.

"Well, my lands, hon," Mother stood up to hug him. "What're you doin' home?"

"I got a break between terms," he replied. "My summer RA job hasn't started so I thought I'd come home for a few weeks as a surprise."

"What's an RA job?" Mother asked.

"I'm a Resident Advisor in Crane Hall for summer school and I'll be helping with stuff like Business Week and Governor's School. It pays my tuition and room and board for the summer."

"Isn't that great? He's paid for his college with scholarships and everything. So, when did you get home?" I asked, trying my best not to sound accusatory.

"Oh I got in a little bit ago. Got an early start from school this morning."

"It's the funniest thing," Mother said, "Your Mama was just talking about you last night. Asking if you were home when they got back from Jackson Springs."

"Really?" Denny answered, "Well let me put my stuff up and I'll talk to y'all in a minute." He left the room in a hurry. Or maybe I just imagined that.

Mother jumped right back in to her story. "What's even worse is when Ida Ruth tried to set her straight and invited her to a WMU potluck supper at the church and she brought whiskey!"

"I guess she had a different take on the Holy Spirit," Finney laughed.

"Poor Ford, that was Ida Ruth's husband, tried to stay away from home as much as possible. You see, decent people just didn't get divorced back then. That's why he joined the Masons," Mother revealed.

"Brick masons?" asked Finney.

"No, Freemasons," Mother answered.

Mac, quiet up to that point, interrupted, "Y'all talkin' 'bout Dr. Boddy? He was into that stuff."

"He wasn't a Freemason," Finney said.

"Well, he gave me a book about it one time. Right smart fella. I always thought he a little lace on his panties, but he was nice enough."

"Mac!" I said, shaking my head. Finney just smiled.

Ignoring me, Mac continued, "Talks about Masons and all that. Had a real interesting thing on Presidents. Said Washington wasn't the first one."

"What?" Finney and I said in unison.

'I can't remember exactly; it's in the bathroom. It's called The Illuminoids or something like that," Mac said, to himself as we all bolted for the bathroom, Goober hot on our trail.

I snatched the book from among the LaVyrle Spencer paperbacks and James Lee Burke mysteries that are housed in the decorative wooden wheelbarrow resting on the windowsill.

We were excited seeing as how the 7th President theory hadn't panned out. Maybe this was our big break. It needed to be as I don't think I'm cut out for this detective work. I was hoping we'd have an answer within an hour, like on TV.

I plopped down on the toilet seat while Finney, Mother, Goober and a very confused Denny crowded the doorway. As our master bath is not the ideal meeting place, I made my way back to the porch, furiously skimming the material. Apparently, from what I could understand reading so quickly, it concerned conspiracy theories from just about the beginning of everything. Nothing though about…there it is!

"It says something about Washington wasn't the first President. Some historians said that John Hanson was technically the first because he was elected something called President of the United States in Congress Assembled. And that was in November 5, 1781. There were several of those before Washington was elected in 1789, named Boudinot, Mifflin, Lee, Gorham, and St. Clair…"

"Who's the seventh one?" Mother practically yelled.

"Somebody named Griffin," I answered.

"What difference does that make?" Denny asked, still unaware of the past few days' goings-on. He knew that Dr. Boddy had died but couldn't get out of work to come to the funeral.

"Oh, sorry, sweetie, Finney, Mother and I are solving Dr. Boddy's murder," I smiled.

"Wait…what? His murder? Nobody said it was a murder. How're y'all gonna solve it? You have any clues? What do you know about being a detective?" Denny asked, looking confused, like he thought we were kidding, but not sure why we would.

Oblivious to the change in the conversation's direction, Mac continued, "I know a man name of Griffin, who owns a store in town. You know him Mama (that's what Mac calls me)."

"That's right," I said, "Jerry and Easter Lynn Griffin own that clothing store in town."

"He's kinda weird but his wife's nice enough," Mac finished.

Finney frowned, "Easter Lynn Griffin is an idiot." I couldn't have agreed more, although I'd never voice it.

"Is she that cute little thing from that dress shop?" Mother asked.

"No, Mama Rain," Denny said, "that's Easter Lily, her daughter. Easter Lynn's a big ugly woman who wears pedal pushers and add-a-pearls." See, I'm not the only one who says pedal pushers. Of course, Denny probably says it because of me. I need to start saying capris so no one will say he's weird.

"She looks like she'd work at Otasco," laughed Finney. "You'd think she'd be well-dressed owning a clothing store."

"There's a difference between being tacky and stupid, Finney," I said.

"Oh, she's both," Denny laughed. "Believe me."

Turning to Mother, I asked, "What do you think?"

"Oh, I agree. She's definitely tacky."

"No, Mother, about looking for clues at Griffin's?"

Finney nodded, "I guess we're headed to town."

Mother said, "I say we do it tomorrow. Everyone needs to take it easy. Why don't we play cards or Mexican Train or watch a movie. Something that doesn't involve guns or naked people."

"How about Steel Magnolias," Finney said. It's her favorite movie. I just love it, too because it rings true, if you ask me. Friendships are funny things and they're hard to come by as you well know. Once you're out of school, it's just you and your family, if you're lucky. Once the kids are out of the house, then it's you and your spouse. That's when you need your friends. I mean, I love Jemma Beth and Nolee, but because they live so far away, we only see each other a couple of times a year now. Growing up, we saw our cousins and aunts and uncles all the time. Georgie, Linda Ruth and Ernette were my cousins and my best friends.

Since Mac and I got married, we've been fortunate enough to have been able to visit as much as we did when the kids were growing up. Madison (Jemma Beth's daughter) is going to be Maid of Honor in Bailey's wedding and that's because Bailey wanted it that way. It's not one of those situations where you're forced to use cousins you either don't know or don't like.

I'm lucky with Finney. When we first met, we just sort of clicked. Although, truth be told, if it hadn't been for her troubled marriage, I don't think we would have gotten so close so quick. She was always looking for an excuse not to be home, so she was always at our house. But I think it's been good for both of us. I try to keep her grounded and help her in her faith and she forces me to be crazy sometimes. Lord help me, I've gone off on another tangent. My mind wanders these days, like you wouldn't believe.

While I was in my little world, Mother, Denny and Finney had decided that we should watch 'Clue: the movie', as it should inspire us.

I really do think it would help and it is a funny movie; one of Denny's favorites. Have you ever seen it? Oh, it's just too cute. It's like the board game, but they're solving a murder in a big old creepy house. It's got Eileen Brennan and Martin Mull and Lenny from 'Laverne & Shirley' and Madeline Kahn. I recommend it.

Of course, since it's movie time, then it's popcorn time. Good thing I always keep a tin full of my homemade caramel popcorn. Yum. Honestly, it's a wonder we haven't all had heart attacks by now, as many sweets as we eat, not to mention fried everything and gravy as a beverage. Southerners are a hardier stock, I suppose.

After the movie, Denny agreed to drive Finney home on the condition that he could pick up Victoria and go to the Sonic. Since it wasn't even 10 o'clock, I agreed and told him to not be too late. We never had to worry about him staying out late. Like I said before, there's not much to do around here. If worst came to worst, he'd be out in someone's field at a party. I don't think he drinks; he's never really said, but I can tell. He has been best friends with Victoria since I can remember. People say that a boy and girl can't be best friends, but I disagree. Denny and Victoria have the best time just talking and laughing. They had a larger circle of friends (Edwin, Breanna, Maggie) who were over here plenty in high school, playing cards, studying, watching movies and eating. But it's always been Denny and Victoria who were inseparable. I guess she's home from school on vacation as well.

Since it wasn't too late, I decided to read a little before bed. I had a new Christian historic romance novel from the Library. I just love all the history and details. I've always liked romance novels, but they just get so graphic and dirty and I just don't like that at all. Nasty makes me nervous.

Mother had turned in before Finney and Denny were out the door, so it was just me and Goober. Mac always goes to bed early, so he can get up at the crack of dawn to do whatever it is he does at 5:00 a.m. I leave him to it. For all I know, he's a dairy farmer. I guess as long as he's happy then I'll just hush.

What I really want to do is talk to Denny, but it's not so important that it can't wait, I suppose. He's a good son and we've never had a problem with him. He's smart and well-liked and a good Christian but I know he deals with a lot. I don't like to pry but I wish he'd talk to me more. He's almost out of college and then he'll be gone. Bailey's getting married next year and with Toby's enlistment in the Air Force, she'll be gone too. It's not like I'm alone

– I have Mac and Mother and Finney, but they don't *need* me like Denny and Bailey do…or did. I guess that's why I agreed to help with all this craziness – I just wanted somebody to need me. I do wish it was something that was within the scope of my abilities, but you take what you can get. Finney needs me right now and I plan on being there for her.

Maybe Bailey will have some babies soon, but she wants to work for awhile, I think. She's studying to be a teacher which I think is wonderful. I always wanted to work with children. I really should go back to school – maybe that'll be my new project. Maybe *I* need me.

The children at church are wonderful to work with but that's only on Sunday. I'd love to teach every day; to explore new things and see old things through new eyes; to see the looks on their faces when they learn to read or their states and capitals. Denny always loved school. Bailey, ironically, was never a big fan. Well, she liked school well enough, but she hated Math so bad you could almost taste it. But she loves teaching the little ones.

I don't want to push her but I want grandchildren now, thank you very much. The more the better. Denny's never really been one to date, so I don't know when I'll get any from him, so the pressure's on Bailey. I would never tell her that and don't you dare say anything.

Chapter 16

From what I understand, after talking to Finney, she was in her kitchen washing dishes to keep her mind occupied. It was around 11:00 not too long after Denny had dropped her off at home. She didn't want to dwell on the events of the past few weeks, so she was on a cleaning spree. Her plant window looked out onto the blueberry patch she and Dr. Boddy had planted on the side of the house, across the driveway. She didn't really enjoy the upkeep, but she did enjoy the conversations she had on her trips to the Co-op for fertilizer and insecticides and whatnot. Plus, it calmed her to look at the plants and marvel that she had actually completed a useful project. Of course, I used her blueberries more than she did, but she was happy enough. She was noticing how life-like some of the growth was when she realized that she was actually seeing someone crouching in her bushes, like they were trying to hide. She instinctively stepped away from the window and told herself she was seeing things. Why on earth would anyone be in her blueberries? She peeked around the edge of the window to make sure the moonlight wasn't just playing tricks on her. No! There they were again! Someone was out there. She squatted, which I'm sure was both difficult and painful and duck-walked over to the garage door to have another look. She stepped into the enclosed area and made her way to the automatic door, which had a row of small windows running across it about chest high. I wonder if her sneaking was the same as when we went on all our investigations? With the cursing. After another look, she was convinced there was someone there. Who would be out there? Surely no one wanted her dead too? What had Noey done to provoke someone to murder him? She hadn't thought about that the whole time. She had just assumed it was some crackpot. She hadn't really given much thought to why someone would want him dead. She had only been focused on who. Was he involved in some sort of illegal activity? Noey never gambled other than the few trips to Biloxi or Vicksburg. And we just don't have mafia around here. Had Noey used their farm for something? Calling it a farm was a stretch. Sure, they had a barn but the only things inside it were some tools left from when Doc Sherman owned the place, years ago. His kids had sold everything 'As Is' to she and Noey and they hadn't made any forays into farming other than the blueberries.

Heading back into the kitchen, she made a mental note to check out the barn tomorrow, but for now she needed reinforcements. That's where I came in. As she was picking up the phone to call me, a shot tore through the darkness and shattered the plant window, the bullet splintering the cabinet just above her head. She screamed and dropped the phone. She grabbed her cell phone and pistol out of the kitchen drawer and scooted to the garage again, as fast as she could. She ran again to the little windows and shot out one of them. She yelled, "You better get out of here! I've called the police!"

She hit speed dial 1 (me) and woke me up from a dead sleep.

"Huh? Wha?" I said, trying to clear my head.

"Cady! Get over here now! Somebody's trying to shoot me!" she yelled.

Shocked into alertness, I jumped out of bed and stammered, "Finney? What did you say? Someone's shooting?"

"Get over here," she screamed and then the phone went dead.

Mac had woken up when I jumped out of bed, one of the pros or cons of a waterbed, depending on the situation, and yelled, "Who's shootin' who?"

"Somebody's tryin' to kill Finney!" I yelled as I threw on my robe and grabbed my purse. Mac jumped up and grabbed his rifle out of the closet and said, "Let's go, Mama." And we ran out the door.

While I waited in the van for Mac to run back inside and put on some pants, I tried to call Finney's phone, but got no answer. I was frantic. Mother, hearing all the commotion, had gotten out of bed and so I asked her to make coffee and pray. Denny hadn't returned from taking Victoria to the Sonic.

Mac jumped in the van and floored it and we covered the two miles between Finney's house and ours in about 2 minutes. I just closed my eyes and prayed for, among other things, safe driving and Finney's rescue. We both scanned the yard as we squealed into the drive. We didn't see anything. Suddenly Finney came running out of the garage, jumped up in the air and fell flat on her back. I ran to help her, confused.

She screamed, "Blueberries!" and pointed toward her little garden and Mac took off with his gun cocked and ready.

I ran to her and asked why she jumped in the air.

"I was trying to do a toe-touch. I thought it might scare whoever's out there."

Trying not to laugh, I said, "Well, I'm sure it worked."

We walked past the front steps to the garage and saw some strange white shapes lying about.

"Oh, they've killed the chickens!" Finney moaned.

"You don't have any chickens, Finney," I said.

"Well, they've killed something. Oh," she cried.

Looking more closely, I said, "They're gourds Finney."

"They've killed my gourds! Wait, I have gourds?"

"Good Mercy, Finney, just get in the house," I said pulling her inside. "We're gonna get shot!"

I sat her down in one of her apple green kitchen chairs (they match her cabinet doors) and got her a glass of water and her first aid kit because her elbows were scratched.

She took my offerings and I started to clean up the broken glass, but she made me stop so I wouldn't 'tamper with the crime scene'.

Mac came inside a few minutes later and said he hadn't seen anyone, but when he was walking toward the house he heard 'the awfulest racket. It sounded like an old pulpwood truck.'

"Now who would be driving a pulpwood truck at this hour?" he wondered.

Without thinking, I said, "Crespo Peterson."

Finney gasped, "You don't think…?"

"I don't know," I answered, "all I remember is that Ms. Malvina said she heard a truck the night Dr. Boddy died. She said it was loud like a pulpwood truck."

"But that could be anybody," Mac said.

"Well, that's what I said to her, but she asked me who did I know that drove a pulpwood truck for their regular car," I said. "And I have to agree with her."

"Yep, I guess you're right," Mac admitted, "most everybody only drives those things when they're workin'."

Finney was just sitting there, open-mouthed, "Why would Crespo Peterson want to shoot me? I only know him in passing. We've never even been introduced."

"I don't know, Finney," I said, patting her hand to calm her. "You can never tell with crazy people. Maybe he thought you were someone else. Or maybe he was drunk and thought he was huntin'."

She looked at me like *I* was the crazy one.

Mac added, "That's true, Finney. Crespo's in the same league as Catfish and Cornbread, except he's not as smart."

"Maybe, but I'm just glad he's gone and I didn't get hurt. I wonder what's takin' Jimbo so long to get here?" she said.

"Did you call him?" I asked.

"Yeah, I mean, oh crap," she frowned. "I told whoever it was that I had called the cops, but I forgot to do it. Will you call for me Cady? My hands are still shaky."

After every volunteer policeman, fireman and National Guard member in the county, and that shameful Gentry Stiles came out and Jimbo took some pictures and statements from everybody, I decided Finney would spend the rest of the night with us. I was too afraid for her to stay here and she didn't argue. Who could blame her? I still couldn't get it out of my mind – what was the deal with the pulpwood truck? Could it have been Crespo? Do you think?

Once we got to my house, Finney decided she'd turn in after I set her up in Bailey's room. Turning as she left the kitchen, she smiled and said, "I'm so glad I have you and Mac. Otherwise I'd have been a gone pecan."

"I know what you mean," Mother said, patting her on the shoulder. "Cady and Mac were my saving grace when Covaletta died."

After Finney exited, I turned to Mother and asked, "Do you know what 'gone pecan' means?" I'd only heard it a few times before Finney started saying it all the time. Lord only knows where she heard it, but it sounds as Southern as honeysuckle, so I go along with it.

"No, but I've learned not to question crazy people, especially in her state of mind."

"Mother, you put up a good front, but I think you secretly care what happens to Finney."

"Fiddlesticks, I don't want *anyone* to die, Sister, even if they are weird."

I smiled, "And people say Southerners hate Yankees."

"Yankees, shmankees, I don't *hate* anybody. It's not Christian to hate. I just don't particularly care for loud, tacky people, that's all."

"You're so benevolent," I said, sarcastically.

"Don't you sass me, young lady," Mother warned, shaking her finger at me.

"I'm sorry, Mother. I'm just a little on edge. You ready for bed? I'm exhausted."

"I think I'll read a little before I go back to sleep. Once I get up, it's hard to lay back down. I've started that new Elizabeth Berg novel."

"Ooh, I want to read it when you're finished. I just love her."

"You need to sleep, Sister. I'll see you in the morning."

"I think we'll have banana pancakes tomorrow. Just as a treat. We've been through a lot."

"Sister, you're gonna *treat* us into plus size clothes. Well, you and me, at least. I think Finney's already there."

"I know, but we've been through so much stress," I countered. Maybe we have eaten too many sweets lately. Nah.

"The only stress I'm feeling is in the elastic of my pantyhose. How about we just have some coffee? There's no need for you to wear yourself out. Now get some sleep."

"It would be nice to sleep in," I sighed.

"Exactly. We need our wits about us if we're going to solve this case."

"I guess you've decided to join our team?" I smiled.

"Team nothing. It's you two running around the county getting into who knows what. But I do need a little more excitement than the Chicken Foot tournament, you know? I may be old, but I'm not dead."

"I don't even think you're old, Mother."

"Now I know you need some sleep. You've gone to talking crazy," she hugged me.

"Good night, Mother. I love you."

"Love you, too, Sister."

Just as I turned to go down the hall to our bedroom, Denny walked in the door.

"Why's everybody up so late? Were y'all waiting on me?" he asked.

"No, sweetheart, we've just had an episode."

"What kind of episode?"

Mother said, "Somebody tried to shoot Finney."

"You're kidding, right?" Denny stammered.

"Nope, sweetie, that's why she's in Bailey's bedroom right now."

"Do y'all know who it was?" he asked.

"Your Daddy went out to see what he could see, but didn't find anything," Mother said.

I added, "He did say he heard a pulpwood truck."

"That's just strange. I wondered what the fuss was all about. When I took Victoria home, we saw all the cop cars speeding through town. We just thought they had found a party to break up or something."

"I just don't know what to think," I said. "This town is going down the tubes."

"Aw, Mama, it's not that bad."

"A murder and an attempted murder in less than two weeks? What do you call it," I said, sharper than I meant.

"I know that," Denny said, "but that's the first bad thing to happen in about a hundred years. The last time I remember somebody dying that wasn't old when Ray Dell Gibbons drowned and that was when I was in eighth grade."

"I guess you're right," I said, hugging him. "I'm just so wound up."

"Who wouldn't be," he said laughing. "My Mother the bounty hunter. Maybe I should call 'COPS' and see if they'll do an episode on you."

Mother started laughing and said her good nights. I hugged my baby boy once more, just for good measure and reminded him that I loved him and that there was still pie or fudge if Sonic hadn't filled him up.

Laughing as he headed toward the kitchen, he said, "All that and psychic to boot. I love you too, Mama."

Chapter 17

Even though Finney was still wound up from the shooting scare, she insisted we try to see if we could find any clues at Griffin's. You had to admire her being so brave, in the face of everything. I mean, if someone were to murder Mac and then try to shoot me at my house, I'd just want to lie down and not get back up. I know we all think we're strong, but when it comes right down to it, I just don't know. Finney seems to have gained new energy from all this. We *have* to find something soon. I don't want our work to be in vain. It's times like these when I pray the most. I don't know if Finney does, but I sure do. It helps me get through everything. Some people say Christians shouldn't be friends with non-Christians but I think that doesn't make much sense. Who better to witness to than a friend? A lot of Baptists would disagree but I don't think that I care. I know I have to be strong in case she needs someone to lean on, but I'm feeling a little antsy. It seems as though the killer/shooter is someone we know and if they know where Finney lives, what's to keep them from finding out she's staying with us? Then again, I pity the poor ignorant soul that pulls a gun on our property. Mac will shoot 'em in a hot minute. Not that he's crazy, mind you, it's just that you can't just go around scaring people and not expect something in return, you know?

Mother had definitely gotten on the bandwagon. She started right in at breakfast the next morning. She was right. That day of rest had done us wonders. Even Finney looked bright eyed and bushy tailed. Well, at least bright-eyed.

Over one of Mac's creations, boneless pork chop omelets and home fries (you just have to try it to believe it), Mother asked, "How do you propose we scout the perimeter? From the roof?"

We all stared.

"What?" Mother said, "I've been watching reruns of 'Lovejoy' on A&E."

Finney patted her on the back and said, "All right, Miss Marple, let's go check it out."

"Miss Marple's not on 'Lovejoy'," Mother said as we took our dishes into the kitchen. Mac will cook, but he hates to clean. Hey, it's an even trade; I've got a dishwasher.

Finney asked, "How would we get to the roof? It's in the middle of the block isn't it?"

"Yeah, but it's two-story, so there has to be some sort of ladder or stairs or something," I said.

We discussed this for a little while longer before realizing that it would be easier just to go and see instead of trying to remember what was where and if we had ever even seen the back of the buildings or anything.

As we were leaving the house, I kissed Mac on the cheek and warned him about frying a flapjack while we were gone. He does that and then leaves a mess and can't understand how I know, with flour covering every available surface. Men. He frowned a little and said, "As nice a fella as I am..."

"Oh hush, you big baby. We'll see you in a little while," I said, getting into the minivan.

"Bring back dinner from the Sonic!" he yelled as we headed out of the driveway.

Griffin's did make the most sense, as far as we could tell, so we made our way toward the parking lot next to the police auxiliary building. After maneuvering ourselves across the intersection, we stood in front of Griffin's Department Store, trying to decide if we could possibly find an alternative path to the roof via the adjacent stores. We had decided, for some reason, that the answers were to be found on high. I'm not sure what we thought we were looking for, but we had to find something. I guess what we needed to do was sit down and think about what on earth Dr. Boddy meant by the sevens, but we had apparently vetoed that idea without even bringing it up for discussion. I think we were getting a bit caught up in the moment, but I wasn't about to be the one to suggest it. So, the roof it was. Unfortunately, Griffin's is sandwiched between *Le Tippy Tap Ecole de Danse* on the left and

Trudy, Maddie, DeeDee's I Love You Shoppe on the right. Yeah, I think it's stupid, too.

I turned to Finney and asked, "Which one looks most promising?"

"You mean which one looks least annoying," she said, not taking her eyes off the buildings.

Mother suggested *Le Tippy Tap* just to keep moving to avoid suspicion.

"Suspicion by who, Mother," I asked. "We're just standing here looking."

"Nobody stands looking in a town this small, Sister. Everybody knows where everything is. There's no need to look."

"Maybe they'll think we're thinking of joining this here church or whatever it is," Finney said, pointing to the sign denoting the presence of Rising Shine Eastern Orthodox Church of Christ in Glory, Inc.

Hurriedly, I said, "Fine, let's go up. Maybe they'll think we're taking a dance class."

Finney agreed, "That's right. You know, I used to take ballet lessons."

"I'll bet," laughed Mother.

"One more smart remark out of you and I'll shove you into traffic," Finney threatened.

"Hey, I believe you can dance. I saw Fantasia," Mother smirked.

I stepped between them and urged Finney onward and upward. As we opened the door leading to the stairs of the dancing school, we heard the instructor, Ms. Yvonne Dulac-Wisconsin, commanding her students in an indefinable accent to '*become* the flower!'

She turned as we entered and said, with more emotion than was necessary, "You *are* pixie elves!"

Mother answered, "I hardly think so."

"You *must* dance, little elves," Dulac-Wisconsin ordered, moving toward us, arms outstretched as if she were about to begin twirling like a hot pink tornado.

"Excuse us, we're just here to observe," I said as civilly as I could to this 60 something year-old woman who looked better in that leotard than I ever had or would.

"You *must* dance," she repeated, moving towards Finney as if to encourage her venture into all things elfin.

"I *must* smack you if you touch me," Finney warned.

Suddenly Mother whispered, "Follow my lead; I have a plan," and she tangoed, by herself, across the room. Meanwhile, all the flowers had stopped 'being' and stared at the sight of three older ladies dancing in street clothes. I could only imagine the stories they'd tell at supper tonight. I just hope none of them recognize me.

I followed Mother's lead using the only dance I could remember, that wouldn't give me a heart attack if I did it - a modified Stroll. I used to be able to jitterbug and do the pony and all the other ones from when I grew up, but my body has not kept up with anything like that since sometime in the 70s. Finney performed an extremely agile interpretation of the Electric Slide. I knew she wasn't really Baptist. I mean, we know how to dance; at least Denny and Bailey do. But Baptists don't dance in public. At least, we're not supposed to or we're at least supposed to feel guilty about it. I can't remember which. I taught my kids to dance at home and I think its innocent fun. Some dancing is nasty, but just don't do that kind and you'll be good to go.

Ms. Dulac-Wisconsin smiled encouragingly, turned to her students and exclaimed, "*See!* You *can* become the dance!"

Our impromptu soul train ended at the door to the far right corner of the studio, which opened to stairs that led to...the street.

"My Aunt Fanny!" Finney spluttered. "This was pointless! Now what?"

"I guess it's over to the I Love You Shoppe," I sighed.

"I'd rather be pistol-whipped," Mother remarked. "The last time I was in there, I saw so many Peter Pan collars, I started to believe I could fly. I'll wait for y'all at the Cotton Bale."

"What's that saying about rats deserting a sinking ship?" I asked.

"Well, eee, eee, or whatever rats say," she grinned. "I'll see y'all later."

And she bounced down the street, leaving Finney and me to deal with the I Love You Shoppe. I should remind her not to order coconut cream pie. Well, since she deserted us, I think it's every woman for themselves.

The I Love You Shoppe is co-owned by, you guessed it, Trudy, Maddie and DeeDee. Trudy is Trudy Jasper, wife of the mayor and one of the privileged few who lives behind the hospital. Maddie is Maddie LeBlanc who I truly believe was asked to join the business so the name would work. She's got money from her husband's settlement when he got hurt offshore, but she doesn't run in the same crowd as the other two. Dee Dee Smandon is the happiest person I've ever met that wasn't affiliated with cell phone sales or a cult. Their store is like a Hallmark sort of, with more cute stuff than you can shake a ribbon-wrapped "good luck" stick at. I'm not making this up. There is such as thing as a "good luck" stick. It's supposed to be for the wedding. I'd never heard of it until a few years ago. Apparently the bride and groom place it on he floor at the reception and step over it for good luck, like crossing the threshold. It seems to be the thing to do around here. I sure hope so; Finney bought one for Marsha Fairfield.

How they stay in business is beyond me, but it seems to thrive. DeeDee's husband owns one of the factories in town and we know about Maddie's money, so that could be the answer. However they do it, good for them.

Finney and I looked at each other, took several deep breaths to combat the cloud of potpourri that encased the front entrance and entered with the anxiety of criminals entering a courtroom. We had no sooner stepped through the Mylar balloon arch when DeeDee Smandon approached us and with all the restraint of a fully-caffeinated Jehovah's Witness, screamed, "It's Hello Kitty's birthday! Yay!"

I made the sign of the cross and Finney asked, "Does Hello Kitty have anything in leather?" as we backed cautiously toward the toy section, hoping to be mistaken for two large stuffed animals. Finney could've passed for a peacock.

DeeDee's eyes widened like the highway they're supposed to have finished five years ago.

"Oh, yes," Finney grinned, "I much prefer How's it Hangin' Kitty any day."

Looking more confused than normal, DeeDee would not be swayed from her sale. "Everything's twenty percent off. Have you seen our collection of edible pottery?"

"Are you real?" Finney asked.

DeeDee smiled harder, if you can imagine that, and giggled, "I'm as real as a country blue wooden goose memo pad, which would look just darlin' next to your phone or on the refrigerator!"

"Well," I replied, more sarcastically than I had intended, "that's something you never see; country blue geese. How original."

"Thanks!" she beamed, literally, "they're two-fer-one!"

Finney's eyes were starting to twitch and it seemed as if she was succumbing to heady scent of preciousness, so I hurriedly lied, "I have seven already. Do you have any stairs to the roof? My friend needs some air."

"Is that the only reason you came in here?" DeeDee asked in the closest her voice would ever come to irritated. You'll notice I didn't say anything about irritating.

"Oh, of course not," I continued lying, "we're doing a panoramic photo of the old post office for the library."

"Oh, okay, then, the staircase is in the back, right beside the scratch-n-sniff wallpaper."

"Thanks. Hope you *do* have a Hello Kitty kinda day now," I beamed as hard as I could, which can be dangerous if you haven't practiced. I may have pulled something.

"You, too!" she squealed, her smile as big as Velberta Stiles' hair and twice as scary. Trust me on this.

Chapter 18

Finney and I followed DeeDee's directions and did in fact find a way to the roof which gave us an unobstructed view of absolutely nothing other than the street and the alley, as Batson's is one story taller than the I Love You Shoppe. We couldn't see onto the roof of the building, not that we thought we'd find anything anyway. What were we doing?

Finney did spot a ladder to the roof and wanted to climb it right away, but I vetoed that idea. Finney is conspicuous in any given situation, but I think people would notice her climbing the ladder. Most of the time people around here don't look up that much as the tallest building, besides the water tower, was First Bank and it was only four stories tall. Plus, the only thing flying overhead would be Lonnie Tack's crop duster. However, people do tend to look sideways and more than likely would've noticed one of us sidling up towards the roof.

We had to make our way back down the stairs to the I Love You Shoppe, but I wanted to just sit. These stairs are something else. Why would someone intentionally climb that many stairs, every day? That stairmaster thing at the gym has got to be a torture device. No wonder all those people look so mad coming out of Lola's Gym. They're tired and can't really decide if it's worth that much work to have a flat stomach, when no one knows what it looks like unless you uncover it in public and decent people just don't do that. I know Finney is ready to pass out, too. But she's a trooper, bless her heart.

I guess I had actually sat down while thinking about wanting to and Finney had as well. I looked over at her and had to laugh. She was apparently arguing with someone in her head because she was making faces and mumbling to herself.

"Hey, Crazy, what'cha thinkin'?" I asked, laughing.

"Oh," she said, blushing. "I was practicing for whenever I have to go see Jerelyn Fortenberry to get my money."

"You can't be mad at her. It's not her fault."

"Not her. Ruetrisha's still in town. Jerelyn said she'd schedule us at different times, but you know how testy demons can get."

Not wanting to go down that road, I said, "We need to go get Mother and get on home."

"I swear if DeeDee says anything weird, I'm gonna snap."

"Just think lots of happy thoughts, darlin', and don't stop moving," I said, pushing her towards the door.

Entering through the back door, we caught DeeDee staring rapturously at a new box of glitter ink pens.

Pointing, Finney said, "That's what happens when you think too many happy thoughts, Tinkerbelle. Let's go!"

I guess one of us must have rubbed against the scratch-n-sniff wallpaper and activated it, because DeeDee suddenly became aware of our presence and ran toward us screaming, "You're back! I knew you couldn't resist those darlin' memo boards!"

Encased in a swirl of strawberry milkshake scented air, Finney stopped and proceeded to clap and sing, "Get thee behind me Satan…" Not knowing what to do, I stopped and kept time with my foot.

DeeDee shouted, "What fun! Whee!" and grabbed my arm and started to square dance. What on earth has happened in my life that I have to keep dancing? I'm Baptist for goodness sakes. I was embarrassed not only to be dancing, with DeeDee or anyone else for that matter, but what if someobody saw, like the Methodists or Marcetta Steeple! I'd never hear the end of it.

I had no idea how to get this dance to stop, so I just dosey-doed DeeDee into a swirling tornado of sequins and hairspray and she disappeared into the stuffed animal section. She reappeared with a life-size Big Bird and as we fled, I could have sworn I heard her singing, "Chicken in the car and the car won't go, Chicago!"

I want to apologize right here and now to that poor Brownie troop I saw headed into the store as we ran down the sidewalk. I just feel terrible.

When we got to the Cotton Bale, I couldn't bring myself to go inside so I sent Finney. Apparently that was a bad idea because after about 15 minutes, they still hadn't come outside so I had to force myself to enter the 'den of iniquity'. I just couldn't stop thinking about the goings on we had unfortunately witnessed and it made me uncomfortable to say the least.

When I finally made it inside and my eyes adjusted, I saw Mother and Finney having coffee and cookies and just laughing up a storm with Ticonderoga Lashley. Everyone calls her Ti (pronounced like tie) and she is somewhat of a local celebrity. Not only is she smart, funny and richer than anybody should be allowed, she used to sing on the Louisiana Hayride with Nolee and had actually recorded a duet with Fats Domino. Through a strategic series of marriages and investments she had accumulated enough property to where she now owned half of Romania. What she didn't own wasn't worth owning, according to her.

I approached the table and Ti looked up. "Hey, Cady, pull up a chair and have some coconut cream pie!" she laughed, slapping the table.

"Yuck!" I said, making a face.

"Oh, Finney filled me in on Mercy's little escapade," Ti said loud enough for anyone to hear. She doesn't care. She'd say it to Mercy's face had Mercy had enough guts to actually get anywhere near the vicinity of Ti's face.

"What have y'all been up to?" I said, testily, "I've been waiting outside for 15 minutes."

"I was talking to, Ti is it?" Mother answered.

"Yes, ma'am, it is, Mama Rain," Ti smiled.

"Then Finney came in and ate all my cookies so I had to order more because I still had coffee left," Mother added. That makes sense, I suppose.

"Finney tells me that she's putting in for the librarian's job," Ti said.

"Yes, we're going to see if the Board will approve the hire if Finney gets her Library Science degree."

"I think I'll give ol' LeLe a call to see if I can grease some wheels," Ti said.

"Are you on the Board?" Mother asked.

"No, that's why I can actually have a little power," Ti laughed. "It's amazing what a simple phone call can do."

"Why're you so interested in the Library all of the sudden?" I asked.

"I love to read and I'm just about up to here with those big ol' ugly volunteers tryin' to tell me I can only check out two books at a time," Ti motioned well above her head.

I decided that since we were here and I don't get to see Ti very much that I'd order something to eat and we'd stay for a bit. When I made the suggestion, Ti was adamant that we leave 'this place of ill repute' and go to her house. Her housekeeper, Flora, was making her homemade peach ice cream. How could we turn down an invitation like that?

We all piled into Ti's 1986 Cadillac Seville. It was a beautiful car.

"Ti, why do you drive a car this old?" Finney asked, as if she didn't drive a 30 year-old car. But I could see her point. Ti was rich.

"When they make another car as beautiful as this one, then I'll buy it. Until then, no thank you. All the cars these days look like bubbles anyway."

We arrived at Ti's house, which is situated just behind the hospital where only a select few can afford to live. Lolly and Bitsy Keene lived next door or the closest thing to next door, which was almost a block away.

"That's close enough to those crazy old biddies," Ti laughed. "I guess they're harmless enough, but Lord knows they drive me nuts, especially when Lolly has one of her spells."

I was concerned, "She has spells?"

"I think she might be getting a little senile."

"Why do you say that?" asked Finney.

"Well, last time she had one, I found her sleeping in my bed and she had the nerve to threaten to call the police when I woke her up."

"Is it that bad?"

"No, Ti's just an old biddy herself," laughed Flora, walking out the back door toward the garden where we were sitting. She was in her late 60s, tall and elegant like Cicely Tyson, but with a fondness for veiled threats and the occasional firearm. Ti came up to her shoulder, but Flora always acted as if she was the shortest woman in town, just because that was the one way to get her goat.

Ti threw her a look and smirked, "You're old enough to be my mother, Flora, so knock it off."

"Mother is the first part of a compound word that I'd like to call you, only company's present." Flora shot back.

"You better watch it or I'll fire you," Ti warned.

"I quit 13 years ago, you big donkey. The only reason I haven't abandoned you is that you're too rich to be left alone. I'm hopin' you'll die first so I can take me a round-the-world cruise."

"You selfish heifer," Ti fumed, "if you think I've been mean before, you wait. I'll ride you like a Christmas pony 'til you drop dead in that messy kitchen of yours!"

"Ooh, big talk for a midget. I'll stomp a mudhole in you. Now do you want ice cream or not?"

"Thanks, darlin'," Ti smiled. "Ladies?"

Mother and Finney were sitting open-mouthed. I forgot how Flora and Ti go at each other, but deep down there's love. Isn't friendship weird? And I don't know what Finney and Mother are so surprised about – they go at each other like tied coons, but I would consider them friends. Not best friends, to be sure, but they seem to enjoy being around each other.

Realizing that I was the only one not fazed by this, I said, "Thanks, Miss Flora, we'd love some. Do you need any help?"

"No, Cady, I'm good. It don't take much to sprinkle poison on her (nodding toward Ti) ice cream."

She left for the kitchen and Ti smiled and said, "So tell me what's been going on? I haven't talked to y'all since the funeral."

I started, "Well, we think that Dr. Boddy was murdered."

"Murdered?" Ti asked, surprised. "In Romania?"

Finney jumped in, "That's what we think, although looking for clues hasn't turned up much."

"Other than some real good gossip," Mother added.

"Well, then all was not lost," Ti laughed.

Flora brought out the ice cream and sat down. "What are you old broads laughing about?"

Ti told her about Mercy and Gentry and Flora made a face. "That's enough to put me off desserts for the rest of my life."

"I'm here to tell ya," laughed Finney, although she sure didn't slow down eating the ice cream. And I couldn't really blame her; there's just something wonderful about a summer afternoon spent laughing with friends eating homemade ice cream.

We sat for several hours and received an education on Romania and its citizens. Ti knows everything about everybody and then some. She was not surprised by what we found out about Mercy and Gentry and offered to buy Tawnette's and fire Ruby Mac for being hateful, which I politely declined. Ti is generous to a fault with her friends and a little bit crazy. She probably would have done it. She is one of a kind, to be sure. She is practically self-made and rich as Croesus. Her parents were successful farmers but she left home to join the Marines when she was seventeen. After serving for a couple of years, she left the military, got married and divorced (I don't think they could handle her), had two kids and started her real estate business in Romania. When her Daddy dies she took part of the insurance money and invested in one of the casinos in Biloxi and made a killing. Then her Mama died and she sold the farm and moved behind the hospital, next to the Keene sisters. She has slowly amassed a real estate empire to rival Donald Trump except with no skyscrapers unless you count the silos of her feed mill.

And she's so generous to the community. She supports the high school marching band and the Dairy Festival through her RC Cola Bottling Plant and gives scholarships to the few local kids who go to college. Denny got a leadership scholarship named after her Mama and Daddy (Lloyd and Emmeline) for being Student Council President.

We were enjoying ourselves, but I knew we needed to get a move on. I had to go home and get ready for the board meeting and I still wanted to talk to Denny.

We said our goodbyes to Flora and Ti drove us back to town to get our cars.

Before she drove off, she put her head out the window and said, "Now if y'all need any help finding clues or spying or just pissin' people off in general, don't forget your old friend Ti." She laughed and roared back toward her house.

Mother and I went home and Finney said she would stop by Shonnie's Stationery to see if her resume was ready and she'd meet me at the Library later. I had to stop by the Sonic to get something for Mac. We had been gone a long time and he was expecting a food, I reckon, since he asked for something. Plus, I was too tired to cook.

When I got home Denny's car was in the driveway. Good, I really wanted to talk to him and not just about him coming home, but we hadn't gotten to spend much time together since he arrived.

Mother went immediately into her room to take a nap – I think the heat had just about taken its toll on her. Ice cream can cool you off, but it can't work miracles. It's still hotter than all get out. Denny walked into the family room as I sat down on the couch. Poor thing was sweating just like his Daddy, which is normal during these unforgiving summers.

"Hi, guy," I smiled. "Sit down and relax with your Mama for a minute."

"Gladly," he smiled, "Daddy's trying to make me do some crazy rock moving work and it's so nasty hot that I about passed out."

"Oh, those rocks can wait. So how've you been? We haven't had a minute to talk since you got home."

"I know, it's been really busy, with y'all trying' to solve a murder and all. I've just been reading some for school and trying to map out my goals for next year."

"Goals for what?" I asked, impressed.

"Well, I'm pretty sure I'm campaigning for Senator and maybe I'll get elected Campus Favorite again, that'd be cool. I'm going to try for president of the fraternity, but that won't be until January."

"That's it?" I questioned, no longer impressed. Don't get me wrong, I think it's wonderful and am proud of his accomplishments. I just wish he'd be more interested in classes than popularity. I don't know –he gets good grades and is in the honor society, but imagine what he could accomplish if he put this much energy into academics. Maybe it's because he never really felt like he fit in at Romania. He was well-liked at school, but has never really fit the 'country boy' mold. Mac just doesn't know what to do with him sometimes. Denny's said that if he didn't look like his Daddy, he'd think he was adopted and sometimes I tend to agree. He and Mac have nothing in common but DNA. The only time Denny has ever been in trouble is for silly little stuff like sneaking out to Sonic for lunch that one time with Victoria and Edwin or refusing to wear socks to school because it wasn't in style – he said. The little sock episode was Denny's only 'real trouble', because Principal Walker, was not having any "no sock wearing shenanigans". Denny was suspended for three days and then decided he was only going to wear colored socks. Who knew my son would be a martyr for the cause of fashion. Mac says he doesn't 'get' Denny sometimes, but that's all right; I do. Denny has never let on that he worried about fitting in or being different, but I knew it bothered him. A Mother knows.

"Well, of course, I *will* choose a major," Denny said.

"I would hope so. That is the reason you're in school, isn't it?"

"I guess," he smiled.

"What?"

"I'm kidding. But, I don't really have a choice, unless I want to be a junior again. But don't worry, I got another leadership scholarship and they upped the yearbook editor scholarship to full tuition. So school will be paid for again."

"Well, that's wonderful!" I exclaimed. How can I second-guess his priorities when everything has fallen into place? So what if he's a little preoccupied with popularity, he still gets good grades.

"So don't worry about me. Everything's just dandy, like always."

"Well, one thing is not dandy," I frowned. "I want to know why you came into town a day early and lied about it. I don't care that you didn't come home right away, but why didn't you tell me the truth? I had to hear it from Ruby Mac."

"What? That old biddy, I can't stand her!"

"Don't change the subject."

"The only reason I didn't say anything was that Jimbo's been callin' me all summer, so excited that he's a cop now and he wanted me to come hang out, so he could show off a little bit. He feels like I think I'm better'n him since I went off to school."

"Denny, sweetie, why're you talking like that? Better'n him?"

"I don't know; it happens when I spend time with Jimbo. He put the red in redneck," he laughed. "Anyway, I figured it would be rude to come home and immediately head out the door to hang out with Jimbo, since it was his night off, so I just kept it to myself. I didn't want anybody to get their feelings hurt."

"I figured it must be something like that," I smiled again. "But where'd you spend the night?"

"We met up with Edwin and Scotty Hartfeld and we all slept at Jimbo's uncle's cabin on the river."

"I hope you behaved yourself."

"When have I not? I'm the most boring person alive."

"You are not. You're just too smart to act crazy."

"I guess."

"I love you, man, you know that don't you?"

"Yes, ma'am," he said, trying not to blush.

"Now go on and get ready for dinner. We're eating early tonight because of the board meeting. Oh, and go drag your Daddy out of the yard or he'll never stop piddling with those rocks."

Chapter 19

I got to the Library early and entered through the side door and tried to adjust my eyes to the light. Someone had beaten me here, which was unusual. It was the special board meeting LeLe had called and I wanted to make sure everything was in place before we got started. I'm not the secretary or anything, it's just that I cannot concentrate unless I know there won't be any surprises and I had to double-check myself since lately I'd been focused on the murder almost to the detriment of everything else, except dessert and gossip. And you've been privy to my little mind wanderings, so you know what I'm up against.

I figured Dottie Figueroa would be here before me as she is as dedicated as I am. Denny says it's actually not dedication so much as it's being, well let's just say uptight. Of course, Dottie is supposed to be uptight – she's the Secretary; it's a mandate. Usually we're the only ones around.

I heard someone walking toward me and as I looked down the hallway, I saw something shiny and began blinking rapidly. This 'light' moved toward me and began to speak. Had I suddenly died and not realized it? Was this an angel? The voice sounded oddly familiar and I realized that it Mary Myra Holstead Newcomb. She was wearing a gold lame' summer sweater, silver stirrup pants and those same bronze espadrilles. What is it with her and those shoes? I felt like singing the Olympic theme song, but I couldn't remember the words. Are there any words?

I'm guessing that LeLe had anticipated a regular length meeting as Mary Myra was in charge of refreshments. Maybe it will go quickly. Billie Shannon hadn't been in awhile and everyone was sure to vote for Finney just to have this problem solved, so it shouldn't take too long.

Mary Myra has always been friendly to me as she mistakenly assumes we are the best of friends by virtue of our Mothers' relationship, which she had discovered several years ago. Apparently, Mother and Elmyra had met at a WMU seminar and had corresponded regularly. Of course Elmyra had started inviting Mother to go on trips with her senior group even before she moved here. And the fact that we're Secret Sisters made Mary Myra want to 'bond'. Mind you Secret Sisters is supposed to be secret until the end of the year party, where you unmask yourself. However Mary Myra just couldn't help herself and sent the first letter on the stationery from her husband Dale's law office. When I told her I had deduced we were Secret Sisters, she just squealed and bought me another gift for "being so clever." Maybe I *am* cut out to be a detective. You think?

Don't get me wrong; Mary Myra is a fine Christian woman. She's just so much more than I need in a friend. Besides, I have Finney, whose personality perfectly compliments mine. I need someone who'll be honest and funny and talk about people when I need to, but not call me a hypocrite when I feel it's inappropriate. I know I ought to be ashamed of myself, but I let me slide sometimes.

"Hon-eee!" she beamed, although not as annoyingly as DeeDee Smandon, "I've the most precious little happy for you! Look! Petit-fours in an edible basket from the I Love You Shoppe!"

"Aren't you sweet, Mary Myra," I said, smiling.

"I brought lemon squares for the pre-meeting mingle, strawberry shortcake for during the meeting and gift bags of fudge and hard candy for take-home happies," she squealed. "It was all I could throw together at the last minute."

"It looks like we made the right choice to head up the Hostess Committee. Finney may nominate you for an award," I laughed.

"She does have a sweet tooth doesn't she? Such a colorful lady. Where is she today?"

"She's having copies of her resume printed up at Shonnie's Stationery."

"Oh, that's right; we've got to decide on a new librarian. I just wonder if we're sure that Randa's going to jail."

"Mary Myra, you were here when she slapped Anne Claire and kidnapped Jacoby. Don't you think she'll be convicted?" I asked.

"Dale said she should plead temporary insanity. I guess I just feel sorry for her. Oh, well, what can you do? What happened to Billie Shannon's nominee?"

Billie Shannon Foster is the wife of Hulon 'Junior' Foster and they own the radio station WRLR. Her nominee for the position, her sister-in-law, had been turned down in committee after Dr. Boddy completed his own background check as Finney had taken a copy of her resume home to read. It turns out that reports of her education had been greatly exaggerated. Billie Shannon was, of course, furious at this 'breach of etiquette' and, after trying unsuccessfully to have Finney removed from the Board, had boycotted all subsequent meetings. Finney was unfazed by this as she considers Billie Shannon a lesser among many.

"You hadn't heard?" I asked, surprised.

"No, I'm out of the loop, so to speak. You know I just do the refreshments. Remember, it was a closed session."

"I'm sorry, I thought you were a voting member," I said, honestly surprised as I thought she *was* a voting member. She should be as hard as she works. I continued, "Well, I'm not one to tell tales, but it only seems appropriate you should know."

"Of course, honey, it won't go any farther than this," she smiled and moved closer.

"Between me, you and that stack of books, Billie Shannon's sister-in-law, Giggy, didn't quite finish her studies at Southern Miss."

"How far did she get?" Mary Myra inquired.

"It seems that when Dr. Boddy..."

"Lord rest his soul," she interrupted, bowing her head.

"Uh, yes, anyway, Dr. Boddy did his own little investigation, he found out that not only did she not finish her degree, but her major was Social Work."

"You mean she never worked in a library?"

"Well," I said, "to be fair she did work one semester as a helper, but that's about it."

"My goodness, I had a work-study job taking lunch tickets in the cafeteria at MSCW, but you don't see me lying to get Blythe Anne's job!" she said.

"I don't think you should count a semester's worth of work for anything," I agreed. "When I was a Nenamoosha at MC, we used to volunteer at the Baptist Children's Home on the weekends, but I never claim to be a Child Development Specialist, even though that was my major for three years."

"What's a Nenamoosha? Is that like a sorority?"

"Sort of. They called them Social Tribes, although I'm not sure if that's still the case, you know with the Indian/native American stuff and all. My roommate was a Nenamoosha, too. We used to have the best fun. Well, you remember Gisela Hubert? She spoke at that luncheon a couple of years ago. They're missionaries in Guatemala, she and my cousin Manny. Remember she told the story of how they met when she came home with me for Thanksgiving break." I need to write her a letter. I really do miss her so much and she's so far away now. I wonder what it would take to go to Guatemala. Oh who am I kidding, I get nervous traveling outside of the state, unless I'm in a car. And Lord knows Finney couldn't take the jungle heat. She jokes that the equator is outside her back door and we're nowhere near as hot as the Amazon. Is that near Guatemala?

Mary Myra said, "Well, I declare. I never knew that. We had clubs like that at the W, except we called them Social *Clubs*. I was a Silhouette. Don't you miss school sometimes?"

"Actually, I was thinking about going back and finishing my degree. I'm only nineteen credits away from getting my Bachelor's. I could easily get my teaching certificate in a year."

"Well, that's wonderful! At least you'd be able to tell the truth on an application," she said, surprisingly snide.

"You seem irritated. What's wrong?"

"That Giggy woman had no business lying like that. I don't take kindly to liars." She looked around and stepped closer to me. "Can I let you in on a little secret?"

"Of course, sweetie," I said, intrigued by this new side to Mary Myra. Maybe she wasn't too much of a goody-goody after all.

"Well, it seems that Billie Shannon and Junior bought WRLR with money Billie Shannon's family made in some pyramid scheme in Arkansas. That's why they don't talk about Billie Shannon's family much."

"No!" I exclaimed, "Are you sure?"

"I heard it from Dale, so I'd say that was as reputable a source as any."

Mary Myra's husband, Dale had worked with the Foster's to get FCC approval to change ownership from the Fairchilds when Buddy died and Audrey moved back to Tennessee.

"I need to have you over for lunch one day real soon," I smiled, genuinely; looking enough like DeeDee to make myself nervous.

"Wonderful, I'll call you," she smiled walking toward the meeting room. "See you in a few minutes. I have to make sure everything's ready."

I stood marveling at this surprising twist when Finney suddenly burst through the door and almost knocked me down.

"Cady! I'm sorry; I didn't see you. Am I late?" she panted as she had apparently run from her car and up the back steps. She pulled her resume from under her arm. They were damp.

Trying to hide my disgust, I said, "So, the ink's still wet, huh?"

"Don't blame me," she pouted, "I never raised my hand to say I was sure."

Chapter 20

We made it into the meeting without any altercations, no thanks to Billie Shannon, who had decided to show up for some reason. I don't know if LeLe told them what the meeting was about or not. I think Billie Shannon just didn't want to miss anything. As soon as she walked in, she saw Finney in the hallway and started loud talking about big women and wind suits and you know she was talking about Finney. I tried to keep Finney distracted with Mary Myra's desserts and it worked.

LeLe motioned everyone into the meeting room and asked everyone to have a seat. Unfortunately, or on purpose – I don't know, Finney was directly across from Giggy, Billie Shannon's cousin. Why was she here? She wasn't on the Board. I guess other people had noticed, too, because the room was buzzing to beat the band.

LeLe looked up and ever so politely asked, "Billie Shannon, do you have a guest?"

"You know Giggy."

"I believe we've met. Hello, Giggy. Can we help you with something?"

Giggy said, "Billie Shannon said I could be on the Board."

"While we appreciate your eagerness to join, Board members have to be voted on during the election every two years. Ms. Marcetta is our newest member," LeLe said motioning to the largest beehive hairdo in three counties. With her hair she was the tallest person in the room. Without it, you'd tell her to go find her Mama. She is a little ol' bitty thing. I'm sorry, I can't stand her. I know it's not Christian; I'm working on it.

"That's just stupid," Billie Shannon interrupted.

"Well, those are the rules, Billie Shannon, you should know that by now." Turning to Giggy, "If you'll excuse us, we need to get started. But if you want to volunteer, talk to Mary Myra outside and she can get you an application."

Giggy skulked out of the room, embarrassed, while Billie Shannon mumbled under her breath, "I don't know why everybody has to hate me and my family."

Finney made a face at her. Great! This will do nothing for Finney's chances.

Not getting sidetracked, LeLe called the meeting to order just as Billie Shannon said, "I hate you, you old fat cow."

"EX*CUSE* ME?" Finney and LeLe said at the same time.

"Nothing," answered Billie Shannon.

"Do you need to go outside and compose yourself, Billie Shannon," LeLe asked.

Finney jumped in, "There's a whole bunch of things that heifer needs to do."

"Finney, you need to calm down, too," LeLe warned as I grabbed Finney's arm.

"I'm sorry, LeLe, everybody," Finney said, looking around the room to, mostly, understanding faces, although you could never tell about Velberta Stiles. I think that's just the way she looks, even when she's happy. Of course, being that she's married to Harlon and mother of Gentry, I'm sure it wasn't all too often.

Billie Shannon said not to worry about her and LeLe went over the minutes from the last meeting and all the other stuff you have to get out of the way before you can get anything accomplished.

She caught me off guard with her statement, "Now, Cady McIntyre has a motion to present before the Board today in reference to our search for a new Librarian. Cady?"

Well I didn't know what to think. I was most assuredly not prepared to say anything other than give my opinion during the discussion.

"Well, uh, good afternoon ladies. Uh, boy weren't those desserts good?" Oh, my mind was blank and Finney was grinning at me like the cat who got the mouse. I couldn't let her down. Lord, give me some words.

"Uh, well, uh I think that since we've been looking for so long and nobody has applied that has a Library Science degree, maybe we need to put somebody in place who can finish their degree in less than a year or so and make that one of the requirements."

Marcetta interrupted, "I agree with Cady. Do you know anybody?"

Surprised, I said, "Yes, ma'am I do have a nominee."

"Oh, I'll just bet you do," smirked Billie Shannon. "Is this what y'all have been cooking up? Trying to get Finney a job behind people's backs?"

"Nobody's been cooking up anything Billie Shannon," LeLe said. "This was an idea presented to me and I thought enough of it to ask y'all for a vote."

"Finney, why don't you pass out your resume," I said trying to ignore Billie Shannon. Would you mind if I referred to her as BS in this chapter? I'm tired of typing her name, because it's so long, and I think BS is more appropriate. I take your silence as consent.

Finney stood up and walked around the room passing out her slightly damp resumes and sat back down to finish her strawberry shortcake.

Everybody grabbed them and started reading like it was the latest John Grishman. I guess nobody thought about whether or not Finney had ever done anything besides be married to that weird English teacher and be my friend. They didn't know that Finney, when Dr. Boddy was pursuing his PhD had taken some graduate courses and, according to Southern Miss, should be able to finish her Master's in three semesters if she went to summer school. I hadn't known either until we came across her transcripts when we were looking for sevens stuff at her house.

LeLe looked up and said, "I guess we need to open this for discussion."

BS immediately chimed in, "I vote no. She doesn't have a Library Science degree."

"Yes, BS, we know, but as Cady said, we haven't had any luck so far with finding someone who does."

"Y'all told Giggy no and she could get her degree," BS said.

I interrupted, "BS, she doesn't even have a Bachelor's yet. She'd have to finish that before they'd even think about letting her into graduate school and then it'd take at least two years."

"Since when are you so up on everyone's education, Miss Know-it-all?" BS said, her face turning red.

"Finney reported it at the last meeting, when we voted on it," LeLe said.

BS shouted, "Why are you always on their side, LeLe? You never take any of my suggestions and you all just hate my family!"

"I don't take sides, BS; I'm just telling you what happened."

"Yeah, right. You always take their side. You all three get on my nerves."

"Oh shut up, BS," Finney said.

"Finney, please sit down," LeLe said. "I don't need you in the middle of this."

Velberta chimed in, "Y'all all need to quit acting like children so we can get this meeting over with. I've got people coming over and I need to get home."

"Well, I think..." BS started to say something.

Miss Velberta cut her off, "You need to hush when grown folks is talkin', young lady." Looking at LeLe, she added, "Let's get this train started."

"Amen," said Miss Marcetta. I'm not sure if she was praying or agreeing or just wanted to be involved. Either way, LeLe took that as her chance to refocus everyone.

"While I agree that we originally wanted someone with the proper degree, I think we can all agree that this looks like the most likely solution."

"I KNEW it!" screamed Billie Shannon. "I'll never vote for that."

"BS, sit down!" LeLe yelled.

"You can all kiss my tail," BS shouted.

Apparently, we were being heard throughout the Library as Ti Lashley stuck her head in the door and said, "What's all the fuss in here? I can't pick out which Harlequin I haven't read with all this racket."

BS whirled around and spat, "You're not a member. GET OUT!"

Ti's face turned dark and she said, "Don't make me whup you right here, you big donkey. I'll buy this stupid building and kick you out."

"I hate all of you," BS shouted.

Miss Velberta said, "Well, what'd I ever do to you?"

LeLe had to shout to be heard and said, "BS, you need to leave! You're not helping one bit."

"Oh, no, I'm not leaving and have you vote for that hateful woman. I'm staying right here," BS said.

"Oh, no, you're not. You are out of order and you know it."

Miss Marcetta said, "BS, you need to calm down, you're going to hurt yourself."

"Oh, shut up, you big haired thing," BS fired back.

"You better watch your mouth," I warned her. "You don't need to say something you'll regret."

"Don't you talk to me like that, Cady McIntyre, I don't care who you think you are," BS screamed.

Ti jumped in, "You had better shut it BS or I'm gonna have to put my foot up your tail."

LeLe shouted, "THAT'S IT!"

We all stopped and looked. Buddy, let me tell you she was flustered. Her face had gotten red and her hair was a bit mussed. We had never had anything like this happen before.

"Let's just table this and see if we can't compose ourselves before the next meeting, agreed?"

Everybody nodded their heads.

"I'm taking that as a yes vote and we're adjourned."

"I didn't vote, yes," BS whined.

LeLe looked tired and said, "BS, you don't want me to say what I want to say right now. Trust me."

Dottie, who had apparently been taking the minutes diligently, piped up, "LeLe, do you want me to type up what was actually said or just paraphrase it."

"Dottie, I think you know the answer to that already. Come on Ti, I need a drink." LeLe, being Methodist, has no aversion to the occasional glass of wine. Ti, with no stated religious affiliations, has no aversion to anything.

"I hear ya, LeLe," Ti laughed and with that they were out the door.

Meeting adjourned.

Chapter 21

After a meeting like that, I decided that we needed to get out of town for a bit. Since the board had decided to table the discussion, Finney needed cheering up as well. Not ones for drinking, we begged off Ti's invitation to head down to that bar out by the river. It's called Sodom and Gomorrah, or something like that. Actually, it's called Sammy's, but you get my drift. Mother suggested a drive down to Franklinton to get some Peanut Butter Cake at Gladysia's, the cutest little teashop with the best desserts ever. Unfortunately the chocolate pie that the hostess, Melly Jo, forced us to sample got us all hyper and talking about still trying to solve the murder and Mother had the bright idea to go back to Romania and scout out Griffin's, since we hadn't actually done that other than to look for a way to the roof.

We drove again to the center of town and pulled into the parking lot behind the courthouse. We were hoping Jimbo couldn't see us. He's not the keenest individual ever but we definitely looked out of place for that time of night. I mean, nobody would drive into town to go walking at night. Mother had decided this time to come along because apparently, Finney and I, left to our devices, were not doing the best job possible. We snuck across the street, or our version of sneaking, which involved Finney (cursing again) and Mother and me on tiptoe. It must be genetic. We were almost to the ladder by the back door of Griffin's where we were going to momentarily hide to make sure we weren't being followed, when Jimbo intercepted us. Not that is was due to his skills as a detective; rather we found him relieving himself behind the dumpster. I didn't think police still walked around town, but apparently they did and Jimbo's bladder was a rascal, causing him to break the law.

Great, how were we supposed to find anything with him snooping around peeing everywhere? We keep hitting these roadblocks.

We stood motionless until Jimbo turned around and near about jumped through his skin. He recovered and said in his most official police voice, "Whatchalldoin?"

We stepped out of the shadows and sputtered, "Uh, well, Uh, hey, Jimbo."

He looked startled and asked, "Miss Cady? Miss Finney? I thought you might be a burglar or one of them homeless guys we've seen around here lately. Why're you out here this time a' night?"

Finney smiled and said, "I lost my tether ball."

I covered my mouth to stifle a laugh and hoped to heaven that sarcasm wasn't a misdemeanor. Jimbo misinterpreted my actions as trying to keep from crying.

"Aww, Miss Cady, don't cry. You ain't done nothin' wrong as far as I can see. I ain't gonna arrest you."

Not wanting to waste his being nice and all, I said, "Oh, thank you Jimbo. We're just so upset. We're trying to solve Dr. Boddy's murder and thought we might look for clues around town."

Finney tried to shush me, but I figured we hadn't had any luck at all and we could use an ally.

"Murder? Are you sure? Sheriff Stiles said it was an accident. Although, come to think of it, one of the guys said he didn't believe that, but Sheriff Stiles said we couldn't really afford an investigation, so we just dropped it."

"Well, we think we can solve it. We have some clues, but thought we might find some more."

Mother interrupted, "Well, I guess we didn't find any. We'll just be on our way."

"All right, ma'am. Y'all have a good night and be careful," Jimbo smiled as he walked toward the police station.

"Mother, what are you doing? We came here to find out what we could. We're not about to go home!"

"Will you just hush and trust me. We're not going home. I just think that we'll make more progress alone, without that big goofy lawman lurking around watching for us."

"Oh," Finney and I said in unison, impressed.

"Now come on and help me get up the ladder to the roof," Mother said, walking back into the shadows.

Finney was looking back at me, still walking and ran into the dumpster. It didn't make a very loud noise, but it was loud enough to alert whoever was still in the store. We heard the door creak open and Easter Lynn poked her head out. We scattered for the shadows.

"Jimbo? Is that you?" she called out, sounding nervous.

Why on earth would Easter Lynn look for Jimbo? He must patrol every night.

"Jimbo?" she said more piercing.

Finney walked out of the shadows and said, "No, Easter Lynn, it's not Jimbo, it's Finney Boddy."

Easter Lynn fainted dead away.

"Well, how's that for a greeting," Finney frowned. "Help me get her inside so we can shut this door."

"We can't go in there," I insisted. "It's breaking and entering."

"Oh hush, Sister," Mother said. "It's only entering. That huge woman did all the breaking when she fainted."

"She's right," Finney added, "we're just being good Samaritans."

"You know, Finney, you and Mother can justify anything can't you," I said disapprovingly. However, Easter Lynn was halfway in the alley and we really did need to make sure she was okay, so I agreed to help, much to my dismay when we actually tried to lift her. We finally rolled her onto her back and Finney asked me to grab her under her arms and drag her inside. I did and didn't realize that I had to hold on her...uh...*chest.* When Finney brought it to my attention, I turned about six shades of red and immediately lost my grip on her body. She fell with a weird sounding thud. Almost like if you threw silly putty real hard on the ground. It wasn't a very pleasant sound. If she hadn't been injured before, she most certainly was now. Fortunately she was out cold and we laid her down by the cot in the storeroom.

I told Mother and Finney to hurry up and do whatever searching they were going to do and I'd stay with Easter Lynn until she came to. Finney smirked and said, "Are you sure that's the only reason you want to be left alone." Of course she stopped laughing when I threw a stool at her and told her to keep her dirty mind focused on the case.

Easter Lynn lay there sleeping like a baby that's been given wine in her bottle and before long I realized Mother and Finney had been gone for almost 30 minutes. Mother walked up just then and reported.

"All I found was ugly overpriced clothes. How does this woman stay in business?"

"I don't know, Mother, I never shop here. I'd rather just go to Dillard's."

"I hear you, Sister. We ought to drive over to Hattiesburg tomorrow. We could use a break and Lord knows that Finney could use a makeover and some new clothes."

"Mother, Finney dresses just fine. Be nice."

"Now, Sister, I'm not badmouthing her, I'm just saying there's always room for improvement."

Finney walked up and asked, "Improvement for what?"

"That wardrobe of yours, dear," Mother smiled.

"What's wrong with my wardrobe?"

"Well, if you don't know, then I'm at a loss for how to help."

"Who asked you for help? We're supposed to be looking for a murderer, not shopping."

"I'm just trying to help you be a better you," Mother said.

"I don't need your help. I'm just fine."

Mother shrugged, "If you say so."

Finney was starting to get angry, "Now look here..."

I jumped in to keep everyone in their respective corners and changed the subject, "So did you find anything?"

"Yeah, a couple of blouses for when you make me go to church maybe, but other than that, nothing," Finney frowned.

Maybe Mother was right, I thought. If Finney likes Easter Lynn's clothes, then she might need to be steered in the right direction.

"Finney? Mother and I thought it'd be nice to take a break tomorrow and go over to Hattiesburg and do a little shopping and eat Chinese. How's that sound?"

"Like fun. Shotgun!" Finney yelled, vying for the front seat. She claims she gets carsick if she has to ride in the back.

Mother jumped up and shouted, "Who's got a gun? Lord, call Jim Bob!"

"Mother, calm down, Finney was just trying to make sure she got to sit in the front seat tomorrow. And his name's Jimbo"

"Well, that's just about the dumbest thing I've ever heard," Mother said, frowning. "Why can't you just ask, like a normal person?"

"Sorr-eee, oh mighty raindrop, I get carsick," Finney pouted.

Mother cut her eyes at Finney and said, "Well I won't be the only one nauseous tomorrow, but it won't be from sitting in the back seat, I promise you. Now come on before that big woman wakes up."

"We can't leave, she saw me out there," Finney wailed.

Mother added, on her way out the door, "Yes, she saw *you*, but not us. Good night."

Hustling Finney out the door before Mother could leave us stranded I asked, "What're you so scared of?"

"Everything," she sniffled, "Noey's death, being alone, being divorced, being accused of Lord only knows what by Easter Lynn tomorrow, paying a lot for a muffler."

"What?" I asked confused.

"I'm sorry, if I don't laugh, I'll scream," she smiled.

"Or sing and nobody wants that," I added.

"Hey!" she pouted.

"Oh, I meant that in the nicest way possible."

Chapter 22

The next morning we slept until about 9 o'clock and then had coffee and biscuits from a can, if you can believe that; Finney was determined to eat something and she had brought these from her house the night somebody shot at her. Sometimes it's easy to tell that she's not Southern. After Mother had denounced the biscuits and, in protest, Finney had eaten them all, we decided to get dressed for our trip. Finney went home to change clothes and get some things; we had decided it was safer for her to stay with us until we could get this solved. At least now Jimbo was helping, although only with the investigation of the shooting.

We had all gotten dressed and were waiting on Finney when Mother remembered she had forgotten her book on the porch and wanted to get it in case it rained while we were gone. She turned to walk outside, saw Two-Dan standing at the door and screamed. I was pouring coffee into my travel mug and almost dropped the pot.

"Mother! What is it?" I yelled, running from the kitchen.

"Sakes alive! We need to get him a bell. He nearly scared me to death," she replied, her hand to her chest.

"Its okay, Mother," I said, opening the door. "He wouldn't hurt you."

"Oh, I know that. I'm just so jumpy since Finney was attacked. I'm starting to go gray."

"What's wrong with a little gray hair?"

"This from a woman who colors her hair."

I protested, "You color your hair."

"I'm not the one talking about the wonders of going gray."

Two-Dan had stepped inside the door, but stood there, looking miserable. He hadn't said anything about macaroni. I'm guessing he was sick of eating it and was afraid to open his mouth. I looked at him and asked if he wanted to sit down. He nodded and sat, looking at me with pleading eyes and whispered, "Macaroni." It was like he couldn't explain himself and we weren't able to figure it out. He seemed to know something, but how to understand it, I didn't know. Somehow none of us were on his wavelength and, sadly, we always assumed it was because *he* wasn't smart.

I couldn't believe he had walked this far again. It had to be eight miles from his house to ours. I'm sure he caught a ride into town, which is not uncommon. Well and still, that's almost three more miles on to here. That's a long way to walk to be misunderstood and force-fed macaroni and cheese. Maybe he doesn't really know anything. Maybe I'm just so desperate to help Finney and feel useful that I'm looking anywhere for anything that makes sense. I need to pray about it and I need to get Two-Dan home.

I decided that since he didn't want food, I would drive him home. I called Finney and postponed Hattiesburg. She said she understood and needed a break anyway. Maybe this little side trip would distract me so I could clear my head. We left the house and as I drove through town I noticed Two-Dan was unusually quiet. I guess he had given up on us. Well, I assumed he was being quiet. I had never really heard him talk until all this macaroni stuff started. We don't travel in the same circles, you understand. Mac and Noe knew him better, but I knew I was in no danger. Otherwise, Mac wouldn't have let me out alone.

When we stopped at the intersection of Boughton and Main, I saw Travis Shelby, President of the First Bank of Romania, and husband of my good friend Lyda, the pianist at Searcy Baptist. They were the sweetest couple and Mac and I often invited them to supper. They were never able to have children, so they sort of adopted Denny and Bailey as their grandkids. We refer to them as Uncle Travis and Aunt Lyda, although they're not blood relatives. In the South, that's a show of respect and affection. Just like when I call older adults like Ms. Malvina, Mr. or Ms., instead of by their first names.

As I was waving, Two-Dan suddenly got excited and started pointing and shouting, "Hanson! Hanson!"

"No, Two-Dan," I said, nervously, "That's Mr. Travis. You know him."

He insisted, "Hanson! Hanson!"

I was beginning to feel very uncomfortable, not knowing if I would have to protect myself if he got too excited. As we turned the corner I almost wrecked because standing right in front of the post office was Crespo Peterson, himself, talking to Junior Foster. What were they talking about? I know that

Crespo rents some land from Junior but I don't think they were talking about the rent, considering the animated conversation that was taking place. I guess Two-Dan saw them too, because he started yelling "Macaroni! Macaroni!"

What was he yelling all these strange names for? Was Crespo or Junior, 'Macaroni'? What if one of them was? Two-Dan was at the school. He would know if it was one of them. I was so excited that I drove well over the speed limit so I could drop him home as fast as I could. I was trying not to be rude, but this was exciting. I don't know why I thought he should be home instead of with me, since he could identify the killer. There's no accounting for sense when you're excited.

As we made our way toward his house, which is several miles outside of town opposite us, we saw Belva Jean Avery on the side of the road waving her arm like somebody wanting some beads at Mardi Gras. I thought she might be having one of her spasms, until I noticed the smoke comin' out from under her hood.

I pulled over and she ran toward my van, looking so relieved.

"Oh, Cady, I'm so glad you stopped," she said.

"Well, of course, Miss Belva, why wouldn't I?"

"Well, you're the first one to stop. I don't know about people these days. And me with a baby."

I had to make myself not laugh, because I knew exactly why they didn't stop. I wonder if she knows that she waves like that. Surely she must. Somebody has had to ask her about it at some point during her 60-odd years on earth.

"Well, I don't know if everyone knows about your baby, Miss Belva."

Surprisingly, while we were talking, Two-Dan had gotten out of my car and began working on her car. After a few minutes, he closed the hood and said, "Fixed!"

This was wonderful as she had just started a conversation about Cornbread that I had no desire to get into.

Sidetracked, she turned and said, "Thank you, Dan-Dan."

He nodded his head, said "Majorette" and walked back toward my van.

She looked funny and said, "Dan-Dan, I'm Belva Jean, not Marjorie", but he was already in the van.

We waved and she waved back either from friendliness or emotion at mistakenly thinking she had been mistaken for someone else or a loud noise, I couldn't tell.

Two-Dan just smiled at me and repeated "Majorette. Hanson. Macaroni." He seemed pleased with himself. Like he had finally put the pieces of he puzzle together for me. I wondered what he was trying to tell me by adding "Majorette" to the equation.

I smiled and started toward home, but I couldn't get it out of my head. Had he just been repeating words because calling Mr. Shelby 'Hanson' didn't make a lick of sense? I know everybody says he's retarded, but when you know something, you *know* it. Nobody is that insistent without a reason. What in the world had made him call Mr. Travis, Hanson? They've known each other for years. Why had he called either Junior or Crespo 'Macaroni'? Why has he called Belva Jean 'Majorette'? What in the world was going on? Oh, I was giving myself a headache.

The name Hanson had triggered something in my brain, though. I couldn't figure out where I had heard that before. I was desperately trying to remember and not get in a wreck, when it hit me. That book! Hanson was from that book; the first President, according to that writer. And Mr. Travis was President of the First Bank or the First President! Had Two-Dan read the book? Had Dr. Boddy read it to him? Oh, I've got to call Finney and we have to go over that book with a fine-tooth comb. The answer must be in there, because Two-Dan knows and he was there on campus with Dr. Boddy when he died. I guess he's smarter than we thought. Unlike most other people, he must've actually paid attention to what Dr. Boddy said. I knew we should've kept reading it instead of going off on all those wild goose chases, like we did.

I dialed Finney's cell phone and as soon as she answered, I shouted, "The book! The answer's in the book!"

"What?"

I explained to her what Two-Dan said about Mr. Travis and calling him Hanson. She sounded excited, but seemed almost preoccupied. I asked her what was wrong.

"Well," she began, "maybe I'm still shaken up from what happened at the house, but I got a note about another emergency Library Board meeting and I don't think it's for real."

"I didn't get a notice. Who's it from?"

"It didn't say, but it said to meet here right now, but I'm the only one here," she answered, her voice breaking up with cell static.

"Come straight to my house. Leave right now. I'll meet you there."

"Oh, wait, here comes somebody, but I can't tell who," she said faintly. Her phone or mine was dying.

"Finney! Get in your car! Leave right now!" I yelled.

"What the...it's Billie Shan..." The phone had gone dead.

"Oh, my God!" I screamed. "Finney?"

I floored the minivan and headed toward the Library. I decided to take a shortcut off Main, Osborn Circle, which is actually not a circle. It's more like a bike path with all its twists and turns. It's where everyone who is anyone lives; that is if you don't live behind the hospital. These are the almost-rich like Ms. Lyda and Mary Myra and Trudy but not DeeDee. She lives in her parent's old house behind the Methodist church. I had to get to the Library as quickly as possible. Not that there's so much traffic in our small town, but you never know when there'll be a tractor ahead of you. This way I could cut through the parking lot of the elementary school, which used to be the old white high school up until the late 60s. The old black high school is now the high school for everybody. I knew the shortcut because we lived about a block away when we first moved here before we built out by the highway. The house we lived in, on Cincinnati Street, was a wonderful old home that they're wanting to turn into a bed and breakfast. Denny always said it was haunted, but I never put much stock in that nonsense. I never felt uncomfortable there. He always did have an active imagination. I'm sorry I'm running off at the mouth, but I talk when I'm nervous.

I screeched to a halt in the parking space next to Billie Shannon's suburban. I saw Finney's big boat of a car, but not either of them. I raced to the back door and yelled her name as loud as I could, considering I was out of breath from fear and all the running. I tried the door and surprisingly it opened.

I snuck inside, but couldn't see anyone.

"Finney?" I squeaked. "Anyone in here?"

"Back here," someone shouted.

I walked toward the voice, which sounded like it was coming from the kitchen. I anxiously approached the doorway. What on earth would I find? It turned out to be Finney with blood on her hands and Billie Shannon with a black eye. I was shocked.

"What happened?" I asked, my eyes as big as the hamburger patty Billie Shannon was about to apply to her shiner.

Finney started laughing as she ran water over her hands. "Well, it's actually kinda funny. Billie Shannon thought she could scare me. She came here to yell at me..."

"I did no such thing," Billie Shannon interrupted, indignantly.

"Yes you did," Finney stated flatly. "Now hush."

Turning to me she continued. "She got out of her truck still mad about Giggy I guess and just laid into me about some sort of pyramid scheme or something."

"I heard about that," I said absently. Looking at Billie Shannon's facial expression, I instantly regretted it.

Ignoring me, Finney finished, "Then she started jabbing me with her old fingers and with everything else that's happened, I had just about had enough and I hit her. In the eye. Hard."

"I can see that," I said, trying not to laugh.

Billie Shannon chimed in, "Then she tried to run away and tripped over me and fell and scraped her hands. And what do you know about the pyramid scheme, Cady?"

"What?" I said hurriedly. "Let's get a look at that eye."

"Don't change the subject," she hissed.

"I'm not changing the subject. Let's get you some more meat."

"Cady McIntyre," she snarled, "I'm warning you."

"Don't you take that tone with me Billie Shannon Foster," I said, as forcefully as I could. "You need to calm down before you say something you'll regret." I had had enough of crazy people.

"It's all your fault," she said, pointing at Finney and starting to cry.

"I know I shouldn't have hit you, but you just don't go pushing people around," Finney replied. "And Cady's right, you need to calm down."

Oblivious to what Finney was saying, Billie Shannon continued, "Everything was fine until your stupid husband started in on Hulon about the programming at the station. Then we had the FCC investigation. It didn't turn up anything, but that leaves a mark on our record. That's why you were so determined to make Giggy look bad; just because the grand Dr. Boddy couldn't get his way."

"What are you talking about?" I asked.

"Her husband," Billie Shannon said, pointing at Finney, "complained that we aired programs that were filled with profanity and that we didn't serve the needs of the community." She rolled her eyes. "Just because Buddy Fairfield called a female dog a b-word on Pet Swap and we wouldn't play that weird music of his." Turning to Finney, she finished, "And you encouraged him."

"How," Finney asked. "I barely spoke to him last year. He *volunteered* to look into Giggy's background. I couldn't have cared less about that stupid music and I don't listen to Pet Swap."

"You both took so much pleasure in telling everybody about Giggy."

"She deserved to be found out," Finney replied, "she lied."

"So what, who doesn't stretch the truth a little? Just how many people in this town do you think have a degree in Library Science? And who would move here from somewhere else? I think you'd've been happy to have somebody who wanted the darn job, seeing as how the pay is so little."

"That's why I agreed to take the job. You don't think I'm smart enough to be the librarian?" Finney asked, defensively.

"Oh, you just think you're better than everybody. You and that husband of yours, God rest his obnoxious soul. Just because he's a teacher with a PhD."

She looked at me with the one eye not covered by hamburger and continued, "And you, Cady McIntyre. Don't think I don't see right through you. I've got your number. Always Miss Sweet Sweet, but I know you're just a gossip, plain and simple. And you know good and well you had this idea of Finney getting the job all along. That's why you sabotaged Giggy."

"Billie Shannon," I stammered, "is that really the way you feel? That's just downright mean. I am a Christian and I am most certainly not a gossip and I don't have the energy to backstab anybody." Well that was just about the meanest thing anyone had ever said to me, although, it didn't hurt my feelings as it would've normally. It's hard to take seriously anything said through hamburger.

"Yes, I do and so do a lot of other people."

"Who?" Finney demanded. "I want names!"

"Well, there's me for one," she started.

"We gathered that," Finney smirked.

"And Giggy and..." she trailed off.

"Anybody else?" Finney asked.

Billie Shannon just sat looking at the floor and didn't answer.

"That's just what I thought," Finney sneered. "You don't like us. Big whoop! We don't like you. And I may be obnoxious, but I am not a snob and Cady's practically 'Gidget got Baptized'. Now get out of here before I really get mad."

Billie Shannon walked toward the kitchen door, turned and said menacingly, "You just wait Finney Boddy, you'll get yours."

"Is that a threat?" Finney asked, glaring.

"You take it however you want to!" she yelled as she stormed out the door.

Turning to me, Finney sighed, "What is her deal? And what was she talking about with that pyramid scheme stuff?"

I looked away, "I'm not supposed to say."

"Don't make me get you a hamburger patty, too."

"Oh, for crying out loud Finney, you know I'll tell you. I just had to get the formalities out of the way."

"Good. Spill."

"Okay. Mary Myra told me that Junior and Billie Shannon bought WRLR with money Billie Shannon's family made in a pyramid scheme in Arkansas."

"You mean like Amway?" Finney interrupted.

"No, it's like those things where you pay $100 and you get people under you to pay and they get people under them to pay. They can't get in trouble because the statute of limitations ran out, but they don't want anyone to know."

"Well, you could knock me over with a wet noodle."

"You know how they are about their image. They hold themselves up as pillars of the community."

"Pillar!" Finney laughed. "Hah! I've got a different six-letter word for those two."

"Finney," I began to admonish, "Wait, I can't think of any curse words with six letters."

"Me either, I just said that to make myself feel better."

"You are insane."

"I know. Now finish your book theory."

"Oh, yeah, we need to get to my house right now. I think the answer's in that book."

Chapter 23

We raced for my house and filled Mother in on my idea based on what Two-Dan had said in town. She agreed that it sounded like a great clue, but we should focus on the Hanson connection before we went off and forgot about it. Just in case we were really grasping at straws based on what someone who was widely assumed to be slow had said.

Finney started reading the book and since only one of us could read at a time, I volunteered to make snacks to help us get our brains kick-started. Mother agreed to help me cook. Since the trip to Hattiesburg was put on hold, she started a conversation about what she would've bought had we gone. She and I do this sometimes. We virtually shop; not online, but in our imaginations – it's cheaper.

I decided to make Pinkerwinks – these little sausage, cheese, rye toast things – because this would require more substantial food than fudge or pie, plus Mac had threatened to boycott yard work if he didn't get something in his stomach that included "meat as a main ingredient".

Skimming the pages, Finney was on the lookout for something, although we weren't sure what. About twenty minutes later, once the Pinkerwinks were in the oven, she swore she couldn't concentrate and gave the book to me. She had decided she would supervise the baking and tasting if necessary.

I started looking for anything, but I didn't know what, either. Wouldn't it be wonderful if the sevens were just there all of a sudden? How tidy. Of course, something like that wouldn't happen. This is not TV after all, where the killer has the foresight to plan and commit the murder, but doesn't have enough sense to take his shoes with him when he leaves for some reason.

I would prefer a quick, tidy solution. A little row of 7s. Just like right there. Right there! There they were! 7777! Well how do you like that? It's the patent number for the wireless telegraph that was given to Guglielmo Marconi. Marconi...Macaroni? Do you think? No, it couldn't be, could it?

"Great day in the morning!" I shouted running to the kitchen, "I think I know who the murderer is!"

"Who?" Mother and Finney shouted from the kitchen.

"Junior Foster!" I shouted back, reaching the doorway of the kitchen, "from the radio station!"

"What? How do you know?" Finney shouted, although by that time we were shouting in each other's face.

I showed them the sevens and reminded them that Two-Dan had said 'Macaroni' at Junior when I was talking him home.

Finney argued, "But you said Crespo was there, too. And we've been suspecting him all along."

Mother added, "That's right. And anyway, that Double Dan person called some man in town Hanson the other day, when I was taking him home. I didn't remember that being his name, but how can you argue with a man who only says a couple of words? You know him Sister; he's that bank president. You know the one that's married to that woman who tries to steal my grandchildren?"

"Mother, don't start that again. Bailey and Denny love you. You could not be replaced."

"See," Finney interrupted what she would call our 'Hallmark Moment' and said, "Two-Dan is calling people all kinds of names that aren't right. You even said he called Belva Jean, Majorette."

"But we can't ignore it. It's got to mean something."

Finney agreed, "Noey always did say that Junior acted like he invented radio. Maybe he had nicknames for people in town. He certainly had some for me. I guess if I'd actually listened to him when he tried to vent, I'd know who and what. Of course, he'd have been dead a lot sooner too."

"I can't believe we solved it," I smiled.

"Now y'all need to hold the phone. Before y'all go calling the papers, what exactly have you solved?" Mother asked.

"Junior or Crespo is the murderer!" I smiled, triumphant.

"Number one, that's two people and number two, what proof do you have?"

"Two-Dan knows. He can identify him for Jimbo," I replied.

Mother sighed, "Sister, if that were the case, then you'd have gone to the police before you came home."

"She's right, Cady, the cops are a pretty sad group, but, even I would have a hard time taking Two-Dan's word. Imagine him trying to convince a jury."

Mother added, "She's right, they'd think he was retarded."

"Maybe he already tried to tell them, but they didn't understand what he meant," I responded. Seeing their looks, I added weakly, "Maybe we can just confront Junior and get him to confess?"

Finney shook her head, "If he's as crazy as that wife of his, he'll kill us too. Besides, people only confess like that in "Scooby Doo" and "Murder She Wrote"."

"You said I had a cardigan and a bicycle. It might work."

"Look here, Wonder Woman, you don't have a lasso of truth so I doubt it."

"Plus, do we know whether that Belva Jean woman is involved. He had a name for her, too, apparently," Mother added.

"I think that's just a coincidence," I said.

"Cady, you can't pick and choose your suspects based on your opinion," Finney said.

"I guess you're right. What do we do then?"

"If you're so all fired sure it's Crisco or Junior, then let's make a plan to catch them or him or whatever," Mother said suddenly.

"A plan like what? We're not Charlie's Angels," I laughed.

"I don't have the hair for it," Finney added.

"I'm being serious," Mother huffed. "We don't need big hair or a lasso; we just need to be smart about it." Looking at Finney and me, she added, "Thank goodness I'm here."

Chapter 24

Mother and Finney had been arguing the merits of our suspects for what seemed like the umpteenth hour. We were starting to sound like we actually knew what we were talking about. We had tried to remember everything we had ever learned from watching every TV show from Barney Miller to Hawaii 5-0. It helped, I guess, that no one had bothered to tell us we couldn't do it, so we were determined.

We needed Denny here to give us the benefit of his brain. He is a very smart boy and he grew up reading Encyclopedia Brown books, so maybe he'd be able to give us a different take. We had to come up with a plan, but since we couldn't even decide which person was guilty it was difficult to try and catch them, unless of course, they tried to kill someone else and no one wanted to go through that again, most definitely not Finney.

"I'm just not sure it's this Junior person," Mother said for the umpteenth time.

"Who else could it be, Mother?" I answered, "All the clues point to him or Crespo."

"Actually, they don't, Sister. You think they point to that Crisco person because for some reason you are convinced it's him. And even though they don't really point to him, I'm willing to listen to anything reasonable"

"I just can't figure out why Two-Dan would mispronounce Marconi, but not Hanson," Finney added. "I know you say he's supposed to be slow, but it's not that hard of a word to pronounce."

"Marconi is an Italian name," Finney said.

"It makes no difference. It's not hard to say. So why's he keep saying it wrong? And what's with the Majorette thing he's saddled Belva Jean with?"

Mother asked, "And which one was he talking about anyway? Crisco or Junior. And how in the world would Belva Jean be involved?"

Finney said, "Mama Rain, his name is Crespo. And maybe Catfish or Cornbread are both involved and he's just connecting them through their Mama."

I added, "Those boys *are* just nasty white trash."

"Catherine Dyanne, you watch what you say!" Mother raised her voice. "You can have an opinion all you want, but there's no need to resort to trash talk." Looking at Finney, she added, "And whatever these people's names are, we can't prove anything so far."

Maybe she was right. I was having my doubts as well, considering how Crespo Peterson seemed to fit into everything except the Marconi clue. We thought he was the one that shot at Finney and we think he might've been out by Ms. Malvina's when Dr. Boddy was killed. Of course, that's just because of the pulpwood truck sound and the fact that we wanted to find the killer so desperately. It just didn't make sense all together, but it was all we had to go on and I was not about to take another trip around the county and try to find more clues. I don't think I can take any more excitement.

Finney chimed in, "Maybe he didn't mispronounce it. Maybe it's not Marconi."

Mother added, "And we don't even know who that is."

"It's Junior Foster," I said.

"How can you be so sure," Mother asked.

"It'd better be him, because I do not have any desire to climb any more trees or dance like an elf or tote Easter Lynn around," I pouted.

"Or see Mercy naked," Finney laughed.

I frowned at that memory and said, "You hush."

"Look here now, let's think about this logically," Mother instructed. "Who else could Dr. Boddy have been talking about? Who else deals with macaroni? Is there a pasta factory around here or an Italian restaurant?"

"The closest Italian place is a Pizza Hut over in Columbia, I think," Finney answered.

"I don't know of any kind of noodle factory anywhere around here," I added.

"Well, fiddlesticks, I don't know what else to do. Maybe we can find another clue in that book," Mother sighed. "Where is it anyway?"

"I think Denny's reading it," Finney answered.

"I'm not surprised, "I said. "He loves to learn new things, just to know. Nobody'll play trivia with him anymore."

Finney asked, "What does Bailey call him, Captain Trivia or something?"

"I think that's it," I laughed. "Hey, I'll bet he finds something we didn't see."

"Speak of the devil!" Mother said, as Denny walked into the living room. This was probably my favorite room in the house. I had gotten a lovely sectional sofa, which was perfect when the kids were home as everybody had a place to sit, even if they had company. The matching recliners, where Mac and I always sat, were so comfortable. Since Mother came to live with us, I had given up my recliner and I now sat on the end of the sofa nearest the French doors to the porch. The brick wall behind the TV gave the room a rustic feel as did the huge fireplace and hearth. I love my hand painted saw above the mantle. It's one of those big ones that two people used to cut down trees and things. Mac gave it to me for Christmas several years ago. I think it's just beautiful. The painting is of Mother and Daddy's old home place over in Alsatia, right across the river from Vicksburg. A man that lives out near Two-Dan painted it from a picture somebody had taken years ago, when they first bought the place. I think I may have been around two years old. I know the living room is supposed to be more formal, but nothing in this house is formal except for the occasional apology.

"Hi guy," I said, patting the seat beside me. "I know you've probably memorized that book by now. Find anything interesting?"

"Did you know that Jimmy Carter was on the Tri-lateral Commission?" Denny asked.

"What's that?" Finney asked.

"Apparently some sort of board governing the world or something. It sounds like it's about conspiracy theories, but it's interesting. Apparently the Rothschild's have always run the planet, from what I can tell."

Mother interjected, "that's just silly. Who are the Rothschilds anyway?"

"I think they invented banks, Mama Rain," Denny laughed.

"Well, did you find anything we can use?" I asked.

"Not really. Who do you think did it?" Denny asked.

Finney began, "We think Junior Foster did it because 7777 is the patent number for the wireless telegraph."

"Yeah, I saw that in there," Denny said.

"As near as I can figure," Finney continued, "Noey had nicknames for certain people in town, like calling your Uncle Travis, Hanson."

"The First President? Pretty cool. Who told you he called Uncle Travis that?" Denny asked

"Two-Dan," I jumped in. "And he's called either Junior or Crespo 'Macaroni'. He's been saying it since Dr. Boddy died and we think he means Marconi."

Finney added, "And Noey always said Junior Foster acted like he invented radio."

Denny looked at us confused.

"It's all we have, humor us," I smiled.

Mother said, "But that Double Dan person keeps saying macaroni, not Marconi, so I don't know what to think."

"Macaroni and Marconi are pretty close," Denny seemed to be thinking out loud. "Maybe macaroni is a messed up Marconi. You know Crespo Peterson is like Mr. Junior except messed up."

I agreed, "He is three kinds of stupid, but what made you say that?"

"I don't know," he answered, "Just seemed to make the most sense."

"That settles it," Finney stated, "We've got to figure out a way to catch them."

"Them?" asked Denny.

Finney said, "We think Crespo was the one who shot at me at my house."

"We do?" asked Mother.

"Yes. Cady and I have talked about it a lot."

"Why would Crespo kill Dr. Boddy and shoot at you?" Denny asked Finney. "Did you even know him?"

"I knew *of* him. Him and that nasty family, but that's about it."

"I just don't know if y'all are right," Mother said. "I know y'all want to solve this mystery so we can all relax around here, but I think you're grasping at straws."

"But he drives the pulpwood truck that we heard," Finney insisted.

"So do a bunch of other people, Miss Finney," Denny said.

"I know, but all the time? Even at night?"

"Well, that's true," Denny admitted. "Most people only drive them at work during the day. None of them ever has a license plate and only about every third one even has a front grill. That can't be the only reason."

"And he's got a gun," I said.

"Everybody's got a gun," Finney added.

"*I* don't have a gun," Mother said.

"Look here Mother of Gidget, you're not everybody."

"It might be him. 'Idiots with pistols' *is* the town motto," Denny laughed.

Finney laughed, "You need to stop, Denny."

Denny protested, "I swear, I have it on a t-shirt."

We all laughed because we had all been on edge for the last several weeks.

Mother asked, "Seriously, don't you think that you'll need more than that to make either of them confess?"

"How do expect to find them?" Finney asked.

"You know Crespo works for Mr. Junior," Denny said. "It shouldn't be too hard."

Finney asked, "Are you sure? I thought they only rented a house from him."

"I went to school with their kids. I thought it was common knowledge."

I said, "Remember, I saw them talking in front of the post office when I took Two-Dan home."

"Well then, we'll need a plan to catch both of them and make them confess," Mother added.

Finney said, "Well, the only place I know Junior would be is at the radio station. As far as Crespo, we don't have the same social director…"

Denny interrupted, "He's probably going to the tractor pull in Platt's Landing."

"How do you know that?" Mother asked.

"Everybody's going. Aren't you?" Finney laughed. "I think I saw you eyeing one of those glittery tractor pull t-shirts Easter Lynn had for sale at Griffins."

Before Mother could get a good swing going with her purse, Mac walked in off the porch and asked, "Hey, Mama, why don't we go eat Chinese buffet for supper over in Hattiesburg?"

"Are you sure you want to drive that far to eat?" I asked.

"It ain't that far, besides, since you cancelled the last trip, it's been so long since we went I think I forgot what it tastes like. I may be forced to overeat," he laughed.

I agreed that we needed some time out of town before our last showdown and we *had* postponed our last trip.

"Denny, do you want to go?" I asked, as he had been so busy visiting his friends that we had just about forgotten he was home.

He laughed, 'Hey, if you're buying, I'm eating."

This is just what we needed. This will give me time to be alone with my thoughts and I could figure out my plan. Oh, we were going to catch Crespo and/or Junior. I haven't given up on that idea. And it's not like talking it over with Mother and Finney and Denny hadn't made any progress, I just prefer to talk things over with myself. It helps me sort though everything better. I'm so much more organized than they are.

Speaking of organization, I just got through wedding out the old clothes in my closet, so maybe a new outfit from Dillard's would be fitting; something in black, perhaps. On a more practical note, I need to look for some slacks. I used to wear Chaus, but they stopped carrying it for some reason and so I had to stop wearing it. And those Born shoes are so comfortable and you can even find them on sale sometimes. Besides, Denny has to go there for his dress shirts. He's a big boy and needs a 19" neck, otherwise, he can't breathe to sing at church. And I love to hear him sing. He got that from Mac. I do pretty well; alto since my hysterectomy. My lands, don't tell Mother I said that. That's what Denny calls an over-share. It just came right out.

Anyway, I play some songs on the piano, but heaven help the church if I have to play anything outside of 'Amazing Grace' or 'When the Roll is Called up Yonder' or that entrance music for Vacation Bible School, which I don't think even has a name. Denny always sings when he's home. I try to get Mac to sing, but he never will. He and Denny sang a duet one Easter that was just beautiful. I wish he could've sung at Dr. Boddy's funeral, but Marsha Fairfield and the Mennonites did a great job. Of course, Deltrenda Walley had the forethought to hide her behind one of those huge ferns they always put out. It wasn't very nice, but I don't even want to think about what Ruetrisha would've said. I mean, we love Marsha but she's hard to watch. Imagine what Ruetrisha would've said, in the holy name of Jericho, of course.

At least she's gone back there now. It was funny. Ruetrisha had sequestered herself in Columbia and we had all but forgotten she was still in town until Jerelyn Fortenberry called Finney to come pick up her check. Finney had asked when Ruetrisha was supposed to be there and Jerelyn said that she had left a number of days before. How about that? Left town without so much as a "thank you". I guess the "Walls of Jericho" isn't a finishing school.

Speaking of finishing schools, I hope that we can help Finney with her wardrobe without being rude. Thank goodness Denny is going. He could charm the rattle off a snake, I swear. We'll definitely need him to convince her to make this big of a change. She's gonna be a hard nut to crack, do you hear me. I mean, she's been dressing like this since I can remember and old habits die hard. Hopefully some of those windsuits will, too.

So off to Hattiesburg we went. Can I tell you that mini-van was full of people? Me, Mac, Mother, Denny and Finney. Poor Goober tried his best to get in, but Mother was too quick. She's spry when she needs to be.

Finney was in the very back seat and yelled out to Mac, "Giddy up, Mac, and somebody pray for the shocks."

"What on earth?" Mother said, looking back at her.

"Well, if I eat more than one helping of Kung Pao Chicken, these bad boys are gonna blow," Finney said, clapping her hands and laughing.

"Well," Mother said, looking appalled, "If we break down, you're pushing, because I am not missing my trip to Dillard's. They're having a sale."

Chapter 25

We made it back from Hattiesburg in one piece, all of us full as ticks and just loaded down with packages. Mother found some really cute stuff on sale. We convinced Finney to try some more subdued colors, with Denny's assistance of course. He actually had her excited about taupe, if you can believe that. Of course, she added a bright scarf and some of her big clunky costume jewelry, but I considered it a triumph. Mother seemed pleased. Then again, she did find a new pantsuit incorrectly marked down to $19.99 instead of $199.99. The manager wasn't too thrilled but she sold it to her for that price. Mother can become quite onerous in the face of what she considers poor customer service and the harried department manager soon realized she was meeting her Waterloo in the Tahari section of Ladies' Petites.

The next morning we decided that we needed to think real hard about Crespo and Junior. Denny agreed that we didn't have much to go on, just some coincidences, but he felt we might have a chance if you exhausted all the possibilities.

We were in the breakfast nook sharing some cinnamon rolls from Tawnette's (I was tired; cut me some slack) when we started from the beginning about what we knew.

First of all there were the sevens that Blythandi had found. Second of all, we felt it was someone who knew Dr. Boddy worked at the high school, which, to tell the truth could have been anybody. Then we thought it had to be someone who knew he would be there late, so they had to know his schedule pretty well. Of course, there was the pulpwood truck we kept hearing at night, which was unusual. It was by Miss Malvina's the night of the murder and we heard it at Finney's the night of the shooting. Then there was Two-Dan saying 'macaroni' the whole time, but not giving us much else to go on. We had found the sevens in that book that told that that was the patent number for the wireless telegraph. Everything seemed to point to Junior Foster including his wife Billie Shannon acting a fool at the Library with Finney. I still thought it was Crespo, but I was starting to doubt myself.

Denny asked, "Do you have any ideas about how to get Mr. Junior to confess?"

"Why just Junior?" Finney asked.

"Well, I've been thinking. If it was Crespo, he wouldn't have been smart enough to think of or pull off anything alone. There had to be somebody that was the mastermind. I figured it must be Mr. Junior."

Mother said, "That's the best idea we've had. If you want to help us, you're hired."

"Actually," I said, "I thought that we could have Ti..."

Again Mother interrupted, "Why do you want to get her in on this?"

"It's the only way my idea makes sense. Plus, I think she'd enjoy it."

"Fair enough," said Finney. "Let's hear the plan."

I filled them in on my idea, which was to have Ti call Crespo and ask him to come over to talk about maybe mowing her yard. If he questions that, she can say that Ms. Malvina had mentioned that he was interested in mowing yards. If she had to lie and say that Lobo wasn't doing a very good job, then she just had to lie. It was for the greater good. While they're talking Ti can let it slip that Finney thinks Dr. Boddy was murdered and that she's performing her own investigation. Then she can let him think that Junior's the suspect because she'll also let it slip that Finney'll be spying on Junior at WRLR tomorrow morning just before sunrise.

Finney interrupted, "Cady, honey, no one is that gullible. He'll never buy that."

"Ms. Finney," Denny replied, "Crespo is just about the biggest idiot that ever drew a breath. When he was in high school, he got mad at his mother so he hit his head against the side of the barn until he passed out. Just so she would know he was mad."

"Who ever heard tell 'o such," Mother scoffed.

"It's true," Denny insisted, "Besides, why would he not believe Ti? People around here think if you're rich, then you're always right."

"That's true," Finney nodded.

"Okay, let me finish my plan," I said. "Jimbo and Denny will be hiding in the woods between WRLR and the Church of the Pearl of the Almighty Saving Dove of Peace parking lot."

"Won't they look suspicious?" Mother asked.

"It's not like there's a nightly patrol. They only have about 10 members," I said.

Denny added, "And Jimbo would be the one to actually patrol it if there was a request."

We all arched our eyebrows.

"He does it as a courtesy; he's not a member," Denny said, rolling his eyes. We all nodded, relieved.

"Anyway, Mother and I will be in the van across the road hidden behind the House of Tires sign. When Crespo tries anything, Jimbo'll arrest him.

"Have you asked Jim Bob and Ti to help?" Mother asked.

Ignoring Mother's continued mispronunciations, I said, "No, but I can call Ti right now. Denny can call Jimbo, seeing as how they're buddies," I answered.

Denny and I left to make our calls, leaving Mother and Finney to sit looking concerned about the plans. They both were afraid of getting shot they said, although I think Mother just didn't want to go. Finney's apprehension was understandable.

We left the house around 4:00 a.m. to make sure we got in place before Crespo showed up. We sat anxiously awaiting the arrival of the now infamous pulpwood truck. Jimbo had agreed to help since the incident at Finney's had convinced him Sheriff Stiles was wrong. He and Denny were hiding out in that parking lot. Mother and I had a perfect view of WRLR's parking lot, but were well hidden by the kudzu.

Around 5:15 we heard Crespo's truck and saw him drive slowly by the station. I don't know why no one thought he'd believe the plan, if he's stupid enough to think he can sneak anywhere in that truck. Crespo's not just dumb; he's that special kind of stupid that's dangerous. Plus, Ti can convince anyone to do anything. How do you think she's so successful?

He drove slowly, but not very quietly down past the station and turned around in Dalbarn Fox's driveway. He drove slowly past again, checking out Finney's conspicuous Town Car, but instead of stopping, he drove on and turned right onto the highway.

There had been a small car following him that I thought was just somebody up early until it followed him both directions. It looked like a boy driving, so it would have been anyone. I think this stake out has me all nervous and suspicious of everybody.

Why hadn't he stopped at the radio station? How could he have missed Finney's yellow Lincoln? You could see that thing a mile away. I was about to call the whole thing off when I saw a figure dart from behind the building toward Finney's car. I forgot the truck stop parking lot sat beside Fox Farms' pasture, which all but encircled the station property. Apparently Crespo had parked by the truck stop and sneaked across the field. Maybe he wasn't as stupid as we thought.

But this figure was a lot smaller than Crespo. What was going on?

A few minutes later, I saw another figure, much larger dart across the parking lot as well. This was turning out to be a party of significant size.

I couldn't tell if either person had a gun or not but it didn't calm my nerves one bit.

Finney was trying to peek inside the windows of the lobby when Crespo walked right up behind her. Finney spun around and screamed. I guess Crespo wasn't prepared for that because he fainted dead away. Suddenly the other figure screamed "Eat dirt hillbilly!' and landed knee-first in Crespo's stomach. It was Blythandi Jeskin! Good Lord, who had told her about this? Jimbo and Denny ran out of the woods just as Junior Foster burst out of the station's front door.

"What on earth?!" Mother shouted.

I floored the mini-van and tore across the road. I couldn't believe that Junior Foster had a gun pointed at Finney while Jimbo had a gun pointed at Junior. Denny was to the side of this little gun circle, trying to revive Crespo. Or whatever you call it when you nudge someone with your foot. Blythandi was squatting by Finney's car trying to decide her next move, I assume.

Something else was drawing my attention. It was Finney. She looked different, weird. What was on her face? It looked like a mask or something.

I started to get out of the van when Mother grabbed my arm.

"Have you lost your mind, Sister? They've got guns out there!"

"But Denny and Finney are out there!" I cried.

"And so is that goofy Jumbo. He's the law; he can handle it. You're gonna get somebody shot."

"Don't you care about your grandson?" I almost wailed.

"He's not gonna get hurt, Sister, he's not even by them," Mother said, pointing. Sure enough, Denny had walked to the other side of Finney's car and crouched down, peeking over the trunk. He had taken Blythandi with him and they were laughing about something.

"But Finney!" I insisted.

"Although she looks weirder than normal, she seems fine. That Junior person can't be dumb enough to shoot her in broad daylight in front of a lawman."

"Well, it's not actually daylight, but I guess you're right," I said, rolling my window down. "Denny!" I yelled. "Come here!" It came out louder than I had intended.

Junior looked in my direction and it gave Jimbo enough time to take away his gun. Giddy up, Jimbo!

Just then Billie Shannon squealed into the parking lot, jumped out of her suburban and ran toward Jimbo, Junior and Finney. Since the danger seemed to have subsided, Mother and I jumped out of the van and ran over to the growing crowd. It was like a tailgate party without the good food.

Billie Shannon had run right up to Jimbo who was handcuffing Junior and shouted, "I demand to know what's going on!"

"Billie Shannon," Junior interrupted. "Why're you here?"

"The alarm went off at home and when I got up you were gone…again," Billie Shannon growled.

Turning to Finney she smirked, "What'd you do, try to break in?"

Finney was incredulous. "To get what? Roy Clark's Greatest Hits? I don't think so."

"Why're you here then?" Billie Shannon insisted.

Denny jumped in, "You're husband and that big lump laid out over there tried to do to Ms. Finney what they did to Dr. Boddy."

"What?" Billie Shannon gasped.

"Oh yes, Ms. Foster," Blythandi smirked. "Attempted murder."

Finney added, "Those violent genes must run in your family."

I interrupted, "What's that in your hand Finney?" I had to know. It was driving me crazy.

Flashing it for everyone to see, she laughed, "Oh that? It's a Noey mask. That's why Crespo fainted. I made it from that huge picture that Shonnie Thornton made for the funeral."

Sniffing the air, Denny added, "I don't think fainting's all he did."

We all grimaced as we had involuntarily sniffed. It smelled like I don't even want to remember, much less talk about.

Finney laughed harder, "I guess his Mother'll be disappointed that he broke that old clean underwear at the emergency room rule. Thanks Noey." She patted the mask.

Turning to Blythandi, Denny laughed, "I think you can thank Blythandi for that. She did one mean karate knee jump to Mr. Crespo's stomach."

Blythandi smiled, "Yeah, the reaction wasn't what I expected though."

"Oh, y'all need to hush," begged Mother. "I can't take much more."

I turned to Junior and said, "We thought you were the murderer."

"Well I'm not," he answered.

"Then why are you here so early in the morning?" Finney asked.

Billie Shannon said, "He comes to work earlier and earlier for some reason."

Junior sighed and said, "Crespo called me and told me what Ti said. It sounded suspicious but I couldn't take any chances. I wanted to get here and make sure I was hiding when Finney showed up. I wanted to see what she thought she knew." Looking over at Crespo, who was still passed out – he must've hit his head when he fainted – Junior asked, "Could we step away from Crespo? The smell's gettin' to me."

Finney laughed, "You'd better get used to it, Junior. You know prison doesn't smell like Bath & Body Works."

Billie Shannon spun around and shouted, "You shut up, Finney Boddy! Hulon didn't do anything!"

Mother whispered, "Who's Hulon?"

"Hulon is Junior," I whispered back.

"Now, you hush, Billie Shannon," Junior said.

Billie Shannon screamed, "How dare you, you ungrateful redneck. I made you who you are, you uneducated piece of white trash!" She lunged for him, "You just wait 'til I get my hands on you!"

"Now Ms. Billie," Jimbo warned stepping between them, "You need to calm down. I know you're upset, but you don't need to say something you'll regret."

"I'm confused," Blythandi added.

"I am, too," I said. "Why are you here, Blythandi?"

"Well, I overheard Denny and Jimbo's conversation because we have a party line with the Jakes' and I decided I wanted to help. I liked Dr. Boddy; he always defended me to those other teachers. Whatever anyone said, I thought he was great. Plus I had already thought it might be that nasty redneck over there," she said, pointing to Crespo.

"Is that what you screamed?" Finney asked.

"Actually I was screaming 'eat dirt hillbilly' but that was just to get his attention."

Laughing Finney said, "I think it worked."

"I'm confused," Mother said.

"You're not the only one," I admitted, "I still don't know who killed Dr. Boddy."

"Junior," said Finney.

"He did *not*!" shouted Billie Shannon.

"Crisco?" Mother said, tentatively.

"Crespo," Denny corrected.

"Whoever," Mother said, pointing, "the dirty one."

"Naw, it's more complicated than that," Junior interrupted.

"What?" we all said in unison, turning to look at him. Was he about to confess? Maybe it *was* like on Murder, She Wrote.

Chapter 26

"So who was it, Junior? You or Crespo?" I asked, still trying to figure everything out.

He sighed and looked at the ground, "No, it wasn't me. It was Crespo. I guess I shouldn't have told him how much I hated Dr. Boddy. I didn't think he'd do something like that."

"Why on earth would you have somebody killed?" Finney asked.

"And how on earth did Double-Dan know?" Mother asked.

"First off, I didn't have anyone killed. When Crespo offered to take care of everything I thought he meant to scare him a little. Second of all, who *are* you?"

"Oh, I'm Rain. Cady's Mother. Nice to meet you."

"Yes, ma'am, nice to meet you, too," Junior said, trying to shake hands while his were cuffed.

Finney sputtered, "Are you kidding me with this?"

"Oh, sorry, Finney," Junior said. "I should've known Crespo would do something stupid. I mean, he's about as bright as a two-watt light bulb."

"You got that right," said Jimbo.

Junior continued, "When I realized what had happened, I panicked. I promise I didn't want him dead, Finney, but Dr. Boddy *was* a self-righteous jerk. He thought he was better'n everybody else. He was always calling the FCC, saying they should shut down the radio station just 'cause we didn't have enough culture to suit him. He wanted a yodeling shepherd or some crap from somewhere and I just flat refused. He wanted to read his stupid poetry on the air and, I've got to think about my audience."

"Nobody wants to hear crap like that," Jimbo added.

"I hate to agree with an accomplice to murder, but Dr. Boddy's poetry was a bit much. No one would have enjoyed it."

"Both of you should watch your mouths," I said.

"Sorry..."

Billie Shannon interrupted, "Dr. Boddy said he was going to try and have the station shut down! Or at least make us sell it!"

"Yeah, that sounds like Noey, all right," Finney sighed. "He liked that Pantupia guy, who knows why."

"Pantupia? What's a Pantupia?" Mother asked. "Is it a flower?"

"I think he's like Yanni, Mama Rain." Denny answered.

"Oh, I just love him and that Linda Evans, too." Mother smiled. "She's got the best hair."

Blythandi looked pained at the last comment and said, "That's it?"

"What's it?" Jimbo asked.

"That's the reason Dr. Boddy was killed?"

"Whattaya mean, that's it?" Finney asked.

Mother asked, "You thought it might be something more exciting than that."

"Somebody was killed because he liked some crappy music? I can't believe that," Blythandi shook her head. "I better turn my stereo down from now on."

I guess we all expected it to be for something bigger or better than that, now that were realized the 'why' in the mystery.

"I want to know why you didn't do anything to Two-Dan," I said.

"Yeah, why'd you shoot at me and not him? I didn't see anything happen," Finney demanded.

"I didn't shoot at you. Crespo did. And I really don't know why either. He stopped telling me what he was doing after I just about beat him to death myself when he told me Dr. Boddy was dead."

"Oh, I'll just bet," Finney added snidely.

"Miss Finney, I promise I never wanted anybody to get hurt. I just wanted to run my radio station in peace. And I never got any. Dr. Boddy gave me crap when I was at work and Billie Shannon gave me crap at home. I wish Crepso would've shot me; I'd have had more fun."

"You ungrateful piece of trash..." Billie Shannon yelled.

"Would you just SHUT UP for once Billie Shannon? Lord love a duck, you don't ever stop talking." Junior almost shouted.

"You got that right," Finney added, daring Billie Shannon to say something else.

"I thought maybe somebody was having an affair with somebody," Jimbo said. "That's what it usually is."

Finney laughed, "Yeah, I'll bet old Billie Shannon secretly had a crush on my Noey."

Billie Shannon huffed, "I'll have you know I have standards. No offense."

"Hey," Finney smirked, "you can drive whatever you like, but automatics are better in traffic."

"Don't be so literal. I meant if I was going to have an affair, I'd pick somebody besides Dr. Boddy."

Mother suddenly waved at the road and yelled, "Look, it's Hello, Kitty!" toward the bubble pink Ford Explorer that had slowed down then suddenly sped up, racing away from the station.

"What does that mean?" I asked.

"What does what mean?" Mother said.

"You said it's Hello Kitty."

"Isn't that her name? I'm just trying to be nice."

"Her name's DeeDee, Mama Rain," laughed Denny.

"Then why does she call herself Hello Kitty?"

"She doesn't. Hello Kitty is one of those stuffed animals she sells at her shop."

"Well, that's just the silliest thing," Mother said, frowning.

I agreed, turned to Junior and said, "You still didn't answer my question. Why didn't Crespo shoot at Two-Dan?"

"He did," Junior admitted. "I guess he didn't tell anybody."

"Mr. Junior, you realize that it's a crime to know about a crime and not tell."

"Yes, Jimbo, I know."

"Did you think you could get away with it?" Finney asked.

"Of course not, but once something's done, you've gotta try to find a way out. I guess I didn't think Two-Dan would remember anything. And I definitely didn't think he'd say anything or at least nothing anybody would listen to or understand. I'll be a monkey's uncle that he did."

Finney added, "I think Two-Dan's just a little slow. Crespo's a full-on idiot. He couldn't turn around without directions."

"I'm not an idiot," Crespo moaned and sat up. We had all forgotten he was there.

"Yes, you are," Finney growled making her way toward him. "You shot at me and killed my husband. I'm gonna kick your butt 'til hell won't have it!"

Jimbo jumped in front of her and said, "Now, Miss Finney, I know you're upset, but don't say stuff like that or I'll have to take you in, too."

"You can't say I'm stupid!" Crespo whined.

"Mr. Crespo, you need to shut up, 'fore I have to use some force on you," Jimbo said.

Billie Shannon yelled, "What are you keeping Hulon in hand cuffs? He's not the killer!"

"Look, Miss Billie, I don't quite know what's goin' on, so just to be safe, I'm arresting everybody that I think should be arrested and we'll sort it out later."

"Well, that's just stupid," Billie Shannon sputtered.

"You need to watch what you say. I don't want to have to take you in, too," Jimbo growled.

Mother added, "Speaking of stupid. Cringo, you *are* stupid if you thought you could kill somebody and get away with it."

"I'm just glad we can put this to rest and it's Crespo," I said.

"Catherine Dyanne, does it matter at this point?" Mother asked.

"I reckon not," I admitted.

"Wait a minute," Denny said. "I want to know why Crespo fainted. It's not like he's not used to a little violence."

"Well, when she turned around and I saw the man's face..."

"See, Noey's face *did* scare you," Finney interrupted.

"Who?" Crespo asked, confused.

"Noey's face. Dr. Boddy? My husband who you killed? I thought it might scare you," Finney laughed.

"I didn't know that was his face. I thought you were one of those he/she/it people from over to Biloxi."

"See!" Mother whispered, "I told you."

"Mother, hush!"

"Let's get this show on the road Jimbo," Junior said getting in the backseat of the police car. "And you better have one of them little tree things or I want to sit up front. Crespo smells to high heaven."

"I got some spray, but why're you suddenly in such a hurry to go to jail?" Jimbo asked.

"Uh, I think I may need protection from Billie Shannon," he chuckled. "I think she just realized I told her to shut up."

We had forgotten about Billie Shannon. We looked over at her and she turned slowly toward us with a look I couldn't even begin to describe. Suffice it to say she was mad.

"Help me, Jimbo," Junior yelled as he jumped in the car before Billie Shannon could reach him with her fist.

"I think that's our cue to leave," Denny said, backing us quickly away from the scene as possible without falling into the culvert, grabbing Blythandi's arm in the process.

Safely inside the van, with the doors locked, I repeated, "Well, I'm glad that's over. All of it."

"I am, too," sighed Blythandi, "but a little disappointed. Some people have no sense of theatre."

"Blythandi, you sound just like Noey," Finney smiled involuntarily.

"Well hush my mouth," Blythandi smiled back.

Mother laughed, "You could take a lesson from this young man, Finney."

Blythandi, looking startled, said, "I'm a girl, Miss...uh... Cady's Mom."

"Really? Well, whatever you are, you sure are cute," Mother said, patting her on the leg.

We held our breaths waiting for what Blythandi would say, although calling Crespo a hillbilly doesn't necessarily make you a bad person. It actually makes you intuitive to a point.

"Well, okay then," she smiled. "No one ever said I was cute, except Mama."

Mother winked at me. Situation averted.

"Let's go home," I said.

"I guess you're coming with us," Denny said to Blythandi.

"I guess so."

We arrived back at our house exhausted from being up so late, but too keyed up from adrenaline to even think about going to bed any time soon. I decided to make some coffee, why I don't know but nobody questioned it so there you go. We sort of just sat there looking at each other listening to Denny and Blythandi chatting away about people they knew and who was dating who and who was pregnant(!) and I don't know what all. It was nice to hear young voices. They're always so full of energy and hope. I had never really known much about Blythandi. Mind you, I know her family and all, but being several years younger than Denny, she was never in his 'crowd' that used to come to the house. I was just sitting there daydreaming and caught myself looking at her. She seems cute enough and very respectful, which is unusual these days; however, we really need to work on her wardrobe. She could be my special project! Someone needs to bring color-coordination back into high schools and society in general, do you know what I mean?

Finney had her eyes closed, dreaming I suppose. Mother had that dazed look on her face that she gets after working in the preschool class during the services at church, and she wasn't talking. Denny and Blythandi's conversation had even trailed off when Finney sat upright and blurted out, "I've got it!"

Let me tell you, we nearly jumped out of our collective skins!

I asked, "You've got what?"

"A solution to the problem."

We sat silent, waiting for her to enlighten us.

Denny ventured, "What problem, we solved the murder."

"Finding a way to remember Noey."

She hadn't mentioned this at all. I wonder how long she had been thinking about this. Lord knows Dr. Boddy would have probably wanted a poetry expo or, at the very least, a statue.

Turning to Blythandi, she smiled, "I'm starting a scholarship in Noey's name and you are the first recipient."

Blythandi sat there shocked. To tell the truth, we all did.

"What? Are you sure?" Blythandi stammered.

"That's awesome," Denny said.

'Well, I figure that you respected Dr. Boddy when most people didn't and you volunteered to help us solve his murder."

I interrupted, "Of course, you didn't tell anyone you were volunteering."

Finney continued, "I think you should be rewarded. Plus Noey really did like you; he was always complimenting you at home. And you know how just didn't do that."

Blythandi nodded, "Yeah, I know. He didn't care for many people around here, that's for sure."

Before anyone could ask, Finney said, "I would have chosen you Denny..."

Denny interrupted, "...but I don't need it. Thanks anyway, Aunt Finney." He reached over to hug her and she beamed as bright as DeeDee Smandon. It was unnerving, do you hear me?

After celebratory glasses of leftover Shasha's Party Punch (its red grape juice, ginger ale and orange slices), I told Blythandi to call her Mama so she wouldn't be worried. After all, someone has to keep everything grounded in reality and I guess that's supposed to be me.

Chapter 27

Blythandi asked Denny to drive her to get her car. Her mother, fortunately hadn't noticed she was gone, so hadn't been worried. Of course, she was most definitely madder than a wet hen, so we said a quick prayer, at Blythandi's request.

Denny said he would go to Tawnette's to see if Two-Dan was there so he could buy him breakfast and then get himself something to eat at Sonic. Did you know they have breakfast? Tater tots at 8 am – Denny is thrilled, let me tell you. And although I was in no condition to cook, I still don't know what I was thinking when I opened the left-over Chinese food for Mother and Finney. I would normally have said that Mother would have been ashamed of me for offering this kind of food to anyone, much less company, but since she had snatched an egg roll and was chewing thoughtfully, I guess I would be allowed this one time. Just don't tell anyone.

"I can't believe we actually did it," Mother marveled as I spooned her some Moo Goo Gai Pan from one of those cute little white boxes they give you. They make me feel like I live somewhere much more cosmopolitan than Romania. Like New York or at least Atlanta. Maybe it's just me. Yeah, it's probably just me.

"I know," agreed Finney. Apparently I was talking out loud the whole time. "I'm just glad we caught the killers and now my Noey has been avenged."

"Is that what we were doing," I asked. "Avenging his death?"

"Well, it sounds good, doesn't it?" Finney asked.

"Sure it does honey," Mother said still nibbling on her egg roll. "And you can have every bit of that Kung Foo Chicken or whatever it is you brought home."

"Why, thank you, Mama Rain," Finney smiled.

"And mind you those things that look like purple hull peas," Mother warned. "I just about ruined my tongue on one last year."

"Ouch!" Finney laughed. "I did that once, too. My whole face stopped working."

"My lands, are they that hot?" I asked, poking around my plate warily.

"It'll knock the color out of your hair," said Finney.

Can I just tell you how good it was to have everybody in one piece? And Mother and Finney seem to be on the best of terms, but I won't hold my breath.

Now that Crespo and probably Junior and maybe even Billie Shannon were going to jail, we could relax. Well, relax as much as possible. Dr. Boddy was still gone and Finney was going to need lots of support, especially now that she was going back to school to get her degree. Oh, did I forget to tell you that LeLe Highsmith-Boone called and said that she had made an executive decision to go ahead with the plan? I believe her exact words were, "...seeing as how a civilized meeting seems out of the question until Billie Shannon is removed from the Board." Oh, but she'll be fit to be tied then. I don't even want to be the one to break the news. Maybe we'll let Ti do it. It'll suit her just fine. I need to call and thank her for her help in our little sting operation.

Won't it be nice to not have to be familiar with words and phrases like sting operation and murder? I'm glad we can put all this behind us. Getting back to normal was foremost on my list of things to do next.

Interrupting my happy thoughts, Mother said, "And that was a nice thing you did for that little girl. Everybody can use money for school." Finney had decided to give Blythandi a scholarship with some of the insurance money.

"I know. I like her; she's got spunk."

"Is that what you call ninja-kicking a hillbilly?" I laughed.

'Well, Noey would've done it if he could have lifted his legs that fast."

"Now that's a nutty idea. I would've liked to have seen that."

Finney blurted out, "Why don't we start our own detective agency?"

I responded, "Speaking of nutty ideas..."

"Are you crazy from the heat?" Mother asked, frowning.

"No, I mean it. We solved this crime. Why can't we solve another?"

I lay my head on the table (I just couldn't take any more) and said, "Finney, sweetie, I know you're overwrought but, number one, we were really lucky about this. You have to admit it wasn't due to our great detective work.

And number two, let's hope that another crime doesn't happen in Romania. I just don't think I can take any more activity like the past few weeks. I'm getting old."

Finney was not to be deterred, "It doesn't have to be here. It can be anywhere. Don't you have a sense of adventure?"

"I left it in my other pants," I smiled. "I'm too tired to think about anything like that. Besides, you're starting school soon. That will take up all your time, as well as the fact that you'll be working, too."

Mother jumped in, "That's right, Miss Astor, you are no longer a lady of leisure."

"I was *never* a lady of leisure," Finney pouted.

"You're right," Mother apologized. "I've never considered you a lady of any sort."

"Don't make me say something you'll regret," Finney smirked.

"Oh, I haven't regretted anything other than letting you in the house that day I thought you were a gypsy," Mother said.

Jumping up to stop that train, I said, "Why don't we just see how your classes go and how much free time you have before making any grand plans."

Finney agreed, "All right, all right, we'll wait and see, but you have to promise you'll help me if anyone asks us to solve another crime."

Mother laughed, "Like that will happen. No one even knows y'all solved *this* crime, honey. Do you honestly think that Bimbo fella is going to give you the credit?"

I interrupted, "His name's Jimbo."

"Jimbo, Bimbo, whatever; he's gonna take credit for solving it since he was the one that arrested them," Mother said.

Finney responded, "You don't know, he might. He'll say something to Harlon, won't he, Cady? I mean, we were there."

"I don't know Finney, and I don't care who gets credit. I just want everything to be normal." I need to put "solve murder" on my list and scratch it off. Then it'll be final.

"Normal!" Mother laughed. "Around here? Are you kidding?"

"Romania is as normal as anywhere else," Finney said.

"I beg to differ," Mother answered. "Alsatia never had stuff like this. The only thing I remember that was even remotely strange was when the Deputy Sheriff punched a horse in the nose and knocked him unconscious."

Finney laughed, "And you call that normal?"

"Well, it was just the one time," Mother said.

"Finish the story, Mother," I added.

"That was the story."

"No, you left out the best part. On purpose I'm sure," I said, turning to Finney. "The man that did it was my cousin Bill Patrick's Daddy, Bill Patrick Jr. – they called him June.

"Oh, so your little town was normal, but your little family wasn't," Finney laughed.

"You hush before I put a switch to those legs," Mother frowned at Finney who was looking at me in that earnest way she had taken on lately.

Apparently she was not to be sidetracked and repeated, "Promise me Cady."

"Promise you what?"

"Promise to help me if anyone asks us to solve another crime."

"I will do no such thing, Finney," I said, not believing she was serious.

Mother chuckled, "Y'all are both overcome with something. That's the craziest thing I've heard and believe you me; I've heard some crazy things in the past two weeks."

"I agree. It's just silly. The last time I promised you something, you almost got killed and I saw things I'd rather have gone to my grave not knowing about."

"But you're my best friend and I'll need you."

I looked at her like she was crazy, which had no effect whatsoever.

"Come on, Cady, promise," she pleaded, looking more sincere than the last time. Maybe she *did* have a heat stroke.

"Fine, I promise," I said. That should be the end of that.

THE END

Big Donkey Fool

(A Sneak Preview)

Although the avocado toilet in her front yard provided a continuity of color often overlooked in the decorating schemes of typical white trash, Marlita Farnham Dufresne wasn't happy with her new station in life. She had always been "dependable and homely", but never trashy and this new label didn't sit well with her, much like the uneven legs on her kitchen chairs.

According to her mother, Javista Steeple Farnham, her "people" from Louisiana had once been the cream of the social crop. Then again, her mother had also tried to convince her that she had been first runner-up to Maid of Cotton in 19whatever. From the wincing looks that so often met her mother when she was in public, Marlita had a hard time believing that story. The Farnhams weren't known for their grace or beauty. What they were known for was, well, it's none of your business and you're rude to even ask.

If you're wondering what made Marlita realize that she was now considered white trash, let me be the first to tell you. Billie Shannon Foster had made the remark under her breath to her sister-in-law, Giggy, after Marlita had accidentally hit them with her buggy near the frozen foods section in the Piggly Wiggly. Marlita had been trying to read the flavors on the Blue Bunny ice cream boxes through the frosted glass and didn't see Billie Shannon who was trying to decide which pie crust to buy, holding the freezer door wide open, causing the glass to frost in the first place. That's Billie Shannon for you; unwilling to make a pie crust from scratch and completely unconcerned with others. Just between me and you, I'm glad someone hit her; I just wish it had been harder. I know it's not Christian, but she's a real piece of work.

Marlita was not the smartest cookie in the cookie jar but she knew enough than to rely on her looks for anything so it came as a surprise that when she began talking about going to college, her less-than-supportive father, Lynch, informed that (1) she didn't need to get any crazy notions about women working and (2) she would marry the first person that asked. In his heart, he truly believed this was for Marlita's own good. But like many good intentions, it invariably went awry. Within a month of graduating high school, Marlita had been married off to a chicken famer named Cletus Dufresne (Doo-freen), of the Shuqualuak (Shook-a-lak) Dufresnes, and had been whisked away to the pre-fabricated world that made up her Camelot. Jackie O, she wasn't. However, she felt that something good had to come out of her life. It had to.

In her voluptuous state, being pregnant with triplets, Marlita was thinking, or rather hoping, that the future would bode well for her little family. She had interpreted the impending children as a sign from God that she would be okay and had decided she should name the girls something biblical like Ruth, Naomi or even Mary; something normal, but biblical nonetheless. However, seeing as how her closest brush with religion encompassed sneaking a cigarette with the Methodist preacher's son behind the concession stand during the Harvest Festival about a month before she was fixed up on the blind date with Cletus, she was stumped for a religious reference. She had gone to church faithfully since she was a child but it never really "took", if you know what I mean. She had never given herself fully to the faith as she was put off by the wailing and screeching and speaking in tongues that so often accompanied the services at the Church of the Pearl of the Almighty Saving Dove of Peace.

Feeling somewhat defeated, she sat alternately napping and flipping through the untold number of channels they received thanks to the satellite they bought from the man in the parking lot of the truck stop. Just because he was selling them from the trunk of his car, didn't mean anything, right? Marlita couldn't believe that at any time of the day or night you could watch an episode of *Designing Women*. What a technological marvel, she would have thought if those words had been readily available in her vocabulary.

She was momentarily jarred awake by the appearance of, well a hooker was what she looked like, but she was clutching a Bible. Maybe she was a reformed hooker. She sure dresses like she's been to reform school, Marlita giggled to herself, blinking to focus her eyes. She assumed she was still too sleepy, as the woman's hair looked hazy. Nope, she finally realized, that's her hair. It's not like Marlita wasn't used to big hair – her mother Javista's 'do was know far and wide, but this woman's hair was whipped into a testament to the homemade meringue sitting high atop a prize-winning dessert; bold, fluffy and white with a tinge of brown around the edges.

Loreen (the woman's name was Loreen Battenfield – it was on the bottom of the TV screen, next to the number to call to donate money - but only if you felt lead by the spirit) suddenly had Marlita's rapt attention when she pleaded for her to "TOUCH the screen!" She assumed Loreen wanted her money...or to heal her – it was what she did, or at least what she said she did. Although Marlita had always believed that "ingrown toenail in Little Rock" was an actual person in need of healing, she herself had never put much faith in these kinds of shows, simply because they had never said her name. Not even that woman on Romper Room saw her in that stupid mirror. She knew she wasn't the only "...and I see Marlita" in the world; she wasn't even the only Marlita in Romania.

Maybe she'll find me some names from the Bible, Marlita silently hoped. As sure as if Loreen had said, "...questioning mother southeast of Hattiesburg", she began citing a verse from 1 Corinthians, Chapter 13.

Loreen solemnly intoned, with the help of appropriate background music and lighting, "...faith, hope and charity. The greatest of these is charity."

"That's it!" Marlita shouted. "I finally found Bible names and aren't they pretty," she gloated, with the triumphant look of one of those people who don't read the fine print of sweepstakes award letters.

"Faith, Hope and Cherry Dee. I like the sound of that."

Cherry Dee Dufresne looked out over the crowd that had gathered around the podium at the town square. The Salsa Festival was the biggest event in Bogue Chitto County and she would reign supreme over the other girls. She liked being the best of the best. The top of the heap. Anything to outshine her sisters, Faith and Hope. Being a triplet was not something that Cherry Dee enjoyed. Sharing gifts with her sisters from unthinking, cheap well-wishers who assumed they only had to give one gift even though there were three recipients did not sit well with Cherry Dee. Daring to imply that she and her sisters had similar tastes was borderline offensive. Faith and Hope were simpletons – Cherry Dee was the star. The Bible said so. "The greatest of these is Cherry Dee." Once her mother had told them the origin of their names, Cherry Dee had felt a sense of destiny. A little annoyed at the spelling, but a sense of greatness nonetheless. And this was when she was in second grade. You can imagine her personality now that she was a rising senior and incoming Student Council President at Romania High. She was also about to be crowned Tomato Queen at the Salsa Fest. Sure she had to share the stage with the Jalapeno and Onion Princesses, but that was a small inconvenience in comparison to the focus that would be on her during the parade. She got to ride in Easter Lily Griffin's Mustang convertible. Faith and Hope had to share the only other convertible in town, a Volkswagen Thing owned by Mr. Carruthers, the woodshop teacher at the high school. And it was orange. Ha! To the victor go the spoils.

There had been rumors that the Jalapeno Princess (Hope) would be elevated to Queen status; the argument being that without jalapenos, salsa wouldn't be salsa. But they would never do that to her. They couldn't. They better not.